Isaiah Light and the Sea of Darkness

A Prequel of the Light the Ark Series –
A Christian Fiction Thriller

James Bonk

Storming Strongholds LLC

Books By James Bonk

Light of the Ark Series

1. Light of the Ark

2. Shadows of the Ark

3. Light of the World

- Isaiah and the Sea of Darkness (standalone prequel)

More Fiction

- Christian's Look Back at Life

Stay up to date on new releases and email exclusive content: https://hello.jamesbonk.com/signup/

To our parents, grandparents, and those who came before us to light the way.
Without your love and work, we would not be who we are
today.

"We are standing on the shoulders of giants."
• Bernard of Chartres

Table of Contents

Chapter 1

Michael's Gift

Isaiah struggled to catch his breath.

Sweat and blood rolled down his face, dripping off his nose into the hot sand that now caked his hands. The last kick had forced all his air out as he gasped to bring it back. Pushing up, he slowly moved off the ground.

"Go ahead, GET UP!"

TTTHHUUDD

Another kick came hard and fast to his midsection and searing pain remained where his ribs were cracking.

Raising one hand to protect his head, he saw Jimmy, his closest friend, lying motionless twenty yards away, blood pooling around his arm and head where two deep gashes were opened.

Jimmy needed medical attention, and so did Isaiah.

The attacker switched back and forth from kicking to pushing with the bottom of their shoe, using it to shove Isaiah. He pushed at his head and shoulders, moving him closer to the busy road ahead of them.

"I knew this day would come," the voice standing over Isaiah said.

TTTHHUUDD

Another kick now came to the head. Isaiah's arm absorbed part of the blow, but the impact to his skull left him dazed as if a grenade went off nearby and stunned his senses.

"You just had to keep asking questions about Joan, then Gary, and then Barbara. You just couldn't accept the answers."

The voice was muffled in Isaiah's ringing ear.

Isaiah felt so naive. All this time, the common thread of all the hurt people. It was right in front of him, but he didn't see it.

He'd underestimated the evil in the world. He thought those involved were looking out for the kids, keeping their interests in line with their own.

How wrong he had been.

This wasn't human nature or self-preservation. This was evil in human form.

It was preying on the young adults of the community. Who knew how many bodies it racked up as it fulfilled its pleasures. There were seven that the police knew about, maybe more they didn't. And now Jimmy and Isaiah were being added to that list.

TTTHHUUDD

Isaiah winced at the pain. He had to stand up. He had to help Jimmy. He couldn't let this evil go on. He had to return to Rebecca. She would be next on the list if he didn't survive.

He struggled to get to his feet as another kick hit his midsection.

TTTHHUUDD

"You want to get up? Go ahead, GET UP!"

Another kick came, not giving Isaiah a chance to get to his feet. Toying with him. Pushing him toward the road.

As he guarded his head against the blows, he realized his Bible was underneath him. He had it when the surprise attack first hit Jimmy and then turned to Isaiah before he could respond. He unconsciously held on to it, protected it, and now still had it through his struggle.

The ancient artifact held in the book's bindings glowed, catching Isaiah's eyes.

If he died, he would never be able to talk to his father about it.

Isaiah knew too much for his attacker to let him live. He was too much of a threat. And Jimmy now knew as well, so he was now in the same boat as Isaiah, floating on the sea of darkness.

If Isaiah couldn't fight back, he would be killed, and the attacker would finish Jimmy off, then move on to Rebecca.

Another push from his attacker's leg, inching Isaiah closer to the busy highway road ahead. Trees and overgrown shrubs blocked the view of the road but the sounds of engines roaring past filled the air as they inched closer.

His eyes caught the Bible again.

In the scramble of the attack, he instinctively protected the book, but as his senses dulled from the kicks, he now saw the glowing light. The light took all his attention. The blows came harder and faster; he was now on the last patch of dirt before a drop to the shoulder, hidden from the cars as they sped past.

"Still can't GET UP?" Tim shouted as he raised his elbow.

Isaiah didn't hear the attacker scream at him or feel another rib break as an elbow dropped on his back, snapping bone.

He was being pulled off the ground so he could be thrown into the road. The busy road with the deceiving turn. The same turn that nearly took Gary's and Barbara's lives.

As the attacker pulled Isaiah up, his Bible and the warm glow gave him strength.

His resolve sharpened.

He had been protecting the book. Protecting the millennia-old glowing gold piece of cherub wing that was hidden in the bindings.

In the chaos of the moment, the book seemed to speak to him. To teach him what he never grasped on his own.

He had been protecting the book, but he was never meant to protect the book.

The book was meant to protect him.

It was his weapon against the evils of this world.

The last seven days were his education, his preparation for the coming fight.

Chapter 2

Seven Days Ago

Isaiah was twenty-eight years old when his father, Michael, decided it was time to pass on the Light family secret.

The year was 1962.

"Son, I want you to have this," Michael said to Isaiah, holding out the worn green family Bible.

"Dad...?" Isaiah said slowly, questioning his father.

The dark blue 1945 Dodge pickup sat running behind Isaiah as his wife, Rebecca, patiently waited in the front seat.

"I wanted to give it to you years ago, but..." Michael paused as his eyes watered.

Isaiah was taken aback. He had seen his father cry but only on rare occasions, and never while saying good-bye to his son. Michael hadn't even blinked when Isaiah and Rebecca moved away from their backwoods rural town to North Florida nearly ten years ago.

Michael was of average height but held a strong presence and seemed to have authority over any room he walked into that made him seem taller than he was. His defined jawline typically held a stern face that Isaiah saw too often during his childhood. Michael rarely needed to punish the young Isaiah for whatever mischief he had gotten into, only to flash his son the stern look and Isaiah knew he had been out of line. However, at times when Michael allowed it, a bright smile would highlight his jet black hair. Michael's smile would beam brightly as he closed every Sunday's service. He led a small, local church and ended his messages the same way for over three decades: "Go in peace, to learn and to love as Jesus would." Michael would say his closing line as he looked to his wife and Isaiah's mother, Leah, and both of them smiled ear to ear.

Michael's black hair had gradually turned salt and pepper and now was nearly all bright grey. His smile and grey hair framed his watery eyes as he held the family Bible out to his son.

"I wanted to give it to you ten years ago, but...but..." The pause was unlike Michael and seemed an eternity to Isaiah.

"There was so much I wish I could teach you, son. But I think...*we* think." Leah stepped up behind Michael and put her hand on his shoulder. He continued, "We think you need to experience it for yourself before I talk to you further about it."

"Dad," Isaiah said, confused and unsure.

Rebecca noticed Isaiah's confusion and stepped out of the truck behind him. Isaiah sensed her, and like Leah gave Michael confidence, Isaiah was bolstered by his wife's presence.

Isaiah reached out his hand to grab the Bible.

In all his time of learning how to lead a church from his father, Bible studies, and devotionals, Isaiah realized he never actually held his dad's Bible before. It was either in Michael's arms or in the top drawer of his dresser. He never left it out, never forgot it at church or on the kitchen table. It was always in his bedside dresser or in his hand.

As his hand unconsciously extended to take hold of the book, Isaiah felt a sensation he never felt before.

His hand flinched as he felt a sudden pain shoot through it, as if pieces of his hand were running from each other, twisted and pulling on a microscopic level within the internal chaos. The brunt of it lasted only a moment, but as he took hold of the book, the pain lit up his whole body like being plugged into an outlet, and a remnant of the feeling lingered within each cell of Isaiah's body.

As the intense pain reduced, a warm feeling took hold. It was a loving, welcoming, pure feeling. Isaiah lost every other sense in his body as he felt the loving warmth take hold of his hand. He felt as if the book was now holding him instead of him taking hold of the book. The welcoming feeling flashed through his body, just as the pain did, but held longer and deeper, finding a home deep within his core.

Rebecca's hand was on Isaiah's shoulder as he held the book, and with a soft tremble of her hand, Isaiah knew she felt the sensation he did.

Isaiah opened his eyes wide, looking to his father without knowing how to respond. His large, hopeful eyes highlighted an otherwise expressionless face.

Michael smiled and released the Bible into Isaiah's full grasp.

The Bible sat between Isaiah and Rebecca on the four-hour drive home. The front of the fixed-up pickup truck felt brighter, as if there was a new glow coming from the holy book and illuminating the couple.

They were visiting their hometown in rural Georgia for a somber event: Joan Auferetur's funeral. Joan was nineteen and lived in the North Florida area not far from Isaiah and Rebecca. Her parents made a similar move as Isaiah and Rebecca, going from rural Georgia to the growing beachside area of North Florida. They lived across town but would come by the Light's church to attend holiday services and stay in touch. Before graduating, Joan attended their weekly youth group and even transferred to the local high school as a varsity swimmer, winning regionals in her junior and senior year and placing top three in states. She also loved to hike and explore, finding solace in nature.

However, one weekend, she left for a hike and never came home.

Her body was found by another hiker seven days later.

Her death shook the local community as well as her small hometown when it hit the papers.

Joan's parents didn't believe the accident story and suspected foul play. When the police wouldn't reopen the investigation, they took their frustrations to the papers. It wasn't like her to go alone or be unprepared but with a lack of evidence and no witnesses, it appeared a tragic accident of falling off the trail and hitting her head on the rocks below. Her parents' frustrations with the lack of investigation ultimately led to their choice to have her buried in their hometown.

As Isaiah and Rebecca drove home, they were quiet for nearly two hours before starting to talk. They didn't talk about the Bible—as miraculous as the feeling was, they seemed to have an unspoken understanding—and Isaiah didn't think he could describe it if he tried. They were more speechless than anything on the subject of that new sensation.

Their conversation started with Joan and shifted to their church and that night's upcoming youth group. The group had grown slowly and steadily in its early years but had seen a spike in attendance in recent years. The increase in attendance coincided with the church leaving Isaiah and Rebecca's home and expanding into a nearby high school gymnasium for Sunday service. The youth group was still hosted at their house every Wednesday, and participation quickly increased as attendance rose in Sunday service.

Isaiah and Rebecca moved to the North Florida coast from rural Georgia ten years ago after getting married.

They first met in the church, specifically Isaiah's father's church during a youth group session. They connected immediately and over time built a shared passion for educating the next generation, especially teenagers going through the difficult transition to adulthood.

Isaiah and Rebecca's bond was forged quickly when both were bullied for voicing their opinion on religion, particularly for loving God's people. During Isaiah's history class, he commented on the harsh treatment of African Americans during the Civil War and likened it to the Jews in Egypt before their exodus. The comment stirred up another boy in the class, who took offense and blamed "those negros," as the boy put it, for the deaths of family members generations ago in the Civil War. Isaiah responded sharply, telling the other boy that his family had no morals, and if they'd enslaved blacks, they likely would have been Nazis if they lived in Germany. A fight broke out and both boys were suspended from school and left with black eyes.

World War Two had ended only five years prior and many kids in the class still held fresh wounds from relatives or parents in the war. War-related comments only magnified the racial comments. The civil rights movement was bubbling but still years away in the 1950 Jim Crow south. Isaiah's comment fired up others in the class, and when a young Isaiah returned from suspensions, he now faced five angry students shouting at him before the teacher could get back control of the class.

Gossip in the small town school spread quickly and Isaiah's comments didn't take twenty-four hours to turn him into a negro and Jew lover. Soon after, he was being called a fairy and pansy. His father's church was his only solace, and even there, he got the sense his peers were merely quieting their insults instead of rebuking them.

Isaiah and Rebecca had met a few weeks earlier and had only been on one date. Rebecca could have easily been scared away or left Isaiah during the incident, but she sided with Isaiah and defended his comments. She was soon labeled with similar names amongst the other girls.

The name-calling blew over within a month or two as the other kids found another topic of destruction, but more than ten years later, the feeling of being an outcast because of their beliefs still fueled the couple. Youth group was an important outlet for both of them to give a safe and secure place for young Christians to meet, make similar friends, and learn about the world.

Most importantly, just as God informed Elijah of seven thousand other believers around Israel in 1 Kings, Isaiah and Rebecca wanted to remind the kids they were not alone.

As Isaiah and Rebecca returned home and unpacked their bags from the trip, Rebecca brought up an issue Isaiah had been trying to avoid.

"Do you think Gary will show up tonight?"

Isaiah stopped and thought.

Gary Freed was a junior at the local high school and his family had been in the church for five years, with Gary attending youth group every week. His parents were also engaged and active in the small church, usually being the first to volunteer in organizing community efforts and potlucks.

A few months back, Rebecca was elated to hear that Gary and Barbara, another longtime youth group attendee, had begun courting. Their friendship was turning into a young romance for the adorable couple. Meanwhile, Isaiah was hopeful that Gary would take up a leadership role in the youth group.

Gary was also quickly becoming the big man on campus. He had all the traits of a well-rounded, respectful young man combined with strong academics and athletics. He took over the starting quarterback job as a sophomore when the first string quarterback was injured and performed far above expectations. The town was abuzz for his breakout junior year for the recent fall season, but the team underperformed and everyone seemed to be deflated. Being the newly hyped QB and then having led the team to a disappointing season, Gary took much of the blame on his shoulders.

Gary had still attended the youth group and Sunday service each week with his family during the season. Isaiah was proud of the young man, noticing that he still had a good attitude and work ethic during the adversity of the rough season.

But soon after the season ended, Gary stopped coming to youth group. A couple of weeks later, his family stopped attending church altogether.

Isaiah remembered Gary bringing a warm and confident presence to the entire youth group. He prayed for the boy to return.

Rebecca's question lingered. "Do you think Gary will show up tonight?"

"I hope so," was all Isaiah eventually replied.

That night, Gary returned.

But not the Gary they remembered.

Chapter 3

No, You Sit Down

"Why do you think the Old Testament shows us the failure and salvation of so many key figures and places?"

The youth group was in the reflection portion of the message as Isaiah facilitated questions and discussion.

The members of the group thought as they looked down or around the room, hoping to draw inspiration to answer the question. Isaiah had learned to let the silence linger instead of jumping in to provide his thoughts. After ten seconds that felt like ten minutes, the thirteen-year-old James Job Jr. raised his hand as he began to speak.

"My dad says it's because it shows nobody's perfect, and also shows what happens when you don't put God first."

"YES," Isaiah exclaimed as he pointed at James, giving him a thanking smile for participating.

James smiled in response. The young man was new to the youth group, only able to attend after turning the minimum age of thirteen. His family was not new to the church, though. Isaiah had known young James since he'd turned three years old. James Job Sr., pronounced like the book of the Bible "*Job*" and not the occupation synonym "job," was the first official member of the Light's church.

Isaiah and Rebecca had a difficult time gaining consistent attendance when they first moved to the area, but after six months, their prayers were answered and they had a returning member. The real estate agent who sold them their house, James Aurelius Job Sr., or Jimmy, as he liked to be called, stopped by to check-in. He was a quiet man, tall and lanky with a large nose and kind eyes. He was mostly passive in his personality but had a strong will that would speak up when needed. Isaiah also couldn't help but notice the various scars on Jimmy's face and forearms that accompanied huge fists. Isaiah sensed those giant fists were not always used for signing real estate papers.

Jimmy had grown up in a low-income rural area outside of the large North Florida town and his passive nature was a testament to the horrors he saw growing up in a broken family and shattered community.

Isaiah and Rebecca were in the middle of a conversation about whether or not they made the right decision by moving, when Jimmy had stopped by to check on them. He apologized for not coming by sooner, but his work, wife, and three children from newborn to three years old had kept him busy.

Jimmy asked how the church was going and how they liked their new home. Isaiah slumped his shoulders during the discussion, but to Isaiah's surprise, Jimmy asked what time service was on Sunday and if it was okay for him to join.

Isaiah had thought that Jimmy must have been as busy as anyone in town: being a real estate agent in a booming city plus three kids and wife at home. It hadn't crossed Isaiah's mind to invite Jimmy to church.

When Jimmy inquired, Isaiah didn't hold back his excitement. "Okay for you join? ABSOLUTELY!"

Jimmy came to the service on Sunday, but to Isaiah and Rebecca's surprise, he did not bring his family. He came alone, and his quiet demeanor held through the sermon, raising his hands and saying "Amen" periodically but in a low voice, barely audible.

He came alone again the next week and the week after that.

After the third week, Isaiah and Jimmy were hitting it off, now talking about the message almost like a Bible study after each service. With no other attendees those weeks, it was easy for an in-depth discussion. Isaiah and Rebecca were hopeful but also confused. On one hand, they were thrilled, Jimmy was the first person that returned week after week, but no one else attended those weeks and Jimmy did not even bring his own family.

As Isaiah and Jimmy wrapped up their discussion, Rebecca couldn't hold back anymore and made sure to ask about his family.

"Excuse me, Jimmy," Rebecca said, "How are your wife and kids doing?"

"Ma'am, you can ask them yourself. They will be here next week." Jimmy had a slight smile as he replied to Rebecca.

"I needed to see this for myself before bringing them along."

In the coming years, after Martin Luther King Jr's *I Have a Dream* speech, Jimmy would tell Isaiah he knew they were itching to ask about his family. Jimmy would also tell Isaiah why he was so protective of them.

He wanted to test the church out himself before bringing his family.

In hindsight, the reason was obvious, Jimmy and his family were African Americans in the 1950s and 60s, right in the middle of the civil rights movement in the deep south.

Many of the area churches did not take kindly to African Americans. Most churches didn't care if people of color sat in the back and remained quiet, but Jimmy was done being passive. He was a hardworking husband and father, growing his business during the day and reading his Bible to his family at night. He figured he had the right to worship the same as any other. He had a right to his religious freedoms. He read his children the Bill of Rights and Constitution at least once a month, discussing how work ethic and morals, not appearance, determined your place in the world.

Jimmy became fed up with passive preachers and his actions would echo the yet-to-be-published *Letter from a Birmingham Jail*. He had dealt with too many indecisive churches over the years and was sick and tired of overhearing racial comments, spoken loud enough so his whole family could hear.

While most people were perfectly fine with their attendance, being kind and polite regardless of their color, the rude outliers of the racists stuck out like a sore thumb. Jimmy and his wife, Dixie, could deal with the fools every now and then, they could even use it as a lesson for their children, but the final straw was when the church's leadership would turn away from it. When they saw it and did nothing about it.

Jimmy decided to start putting pastors to the test, sitting in the front row. He knew someone would comment about "a colored" sitting up front, and Jimmy waited to see what example the pastor set.

Unfortunately, most of the pastors would remain silent whenever they were in earshot of the racial comments, not wanting to rebuke the offending person. When silence rang like a bell in Jimmy's ear, he had his answer, his cue to leave.

He never made a scene.

He simply never came back.

The Job family began doing in-home Bible studies as a placeholder until they found the right place for his family to freely worship. Jimmy's regular attendance at Isaiah and Rebecca's church was not only a relief to the new church leaders, it was an answer to Jimmy's prayers. He saw caring and strong morals in the couple, trusting them enough to bring back his family and make this their official church.

Jimmy cherished the new couple just as much as they cherished him.

Isaiah beamed with joy now, seeing the next generation of Jobs come up in their church.

Back at youth group, Isaiah elaborated on young James Jr.'s response as Rebecca heard a car pull up. She sat in the back of the large living room near the front door of the house. It was her normal seat every Wednesday, and it allowed her to sneak in quietly from the kitchen after she and a couple of girls cleaned up the light dinner that typically started the night.

Her curiosity led her to the front window near the front door.

As she approached, there was a sound from the handle, as if someone was pushing against a locked door.

She paused just in time to avoid being hit by the door as it violently swung open from a hard push.

Gary stumbled into the room.

The smell of whiskey immediately overtook the room as the noise from the crashing door ripped all attention from the discussion and focused it on the seventeen-year-old boy, now on one knee after barging into the room.

"*Weers Bar-ba.*" Gary angrily spit the words out as he slurred the question.

The room looked on in a quiet shock as Isaiah moved swiftly toward the boy. He flashed a glance at Rebecca to confirm she was okay and she assured him with a nod as she too moved in between the children and Gary.

Isaiah knelt on one knee, coming face-to-face with the young man.

Gary couldn't meet his eyes.

The boy's body was there, but Isaiah could see his mind and control were gone, locked away in the back of his mind by the alcohol.

"It's okay now, son," Isaiah tried to calm him.

"*WEERS BAR-BA,*" Gary screamed as his tone shifted away from his original anger to one of fear. His eyes darted around the room, unable to focus.

"Barbara? Do you mean Barbara?" Isaiah said to the boy. "She didn't come tonight, Gary. Tell me where you came from. What do you want with Barbara?"

Gary's mindless swaying back and forth stopped as he heard Barbara was not at youth group. His eyes finally found Isaiah's and their gaze struck him with immense pity. Isaiah couldn't tell if he was scared or confused, but the look of horror on Gary's face etched into Isaiah's mind.

"Sees not...NOT HEEERRREEE?"

Gary's watery eyes could have shed a tear as his expression of sadness conflicted with horror and anger in his drunken state. The raging emotions and alcohol seemed to be pulling his mind apart.

"Come on, Gary, you need to sit down," Isaiah said as he grabbed Gary's arms, softly motioning him to a nearby chair.

"NO! YOU SIT DONE," Gary screamed and jumped back, now at his feet in the open door frame he'd previously kicked open.

"Sees with, sees with..." Gary trailed off. His look of horror turned to disgust as he held both hands tightly on his ears, trying to block whatever voices were overtaking his head.

"Gary, come on in and talk to..."

"NO! You don't, you dot." Gary's slurs took over his voice as he turned out of the house and began running toward the street. He swayed and stumbled as he ran past his still-running car, his family's 1950s station wagon. The driver-side door sat open as the wagon was parked half across the driveway and half still in the road.

Isaiah leaped out of the house and followed Gary as he ran down the street and into the woods.

Chapter 4

Into The Woods

Isaiah pursued Gary over an hour before the boy slowed and collapsed to the ground. The first mile on the side of the road was quick, but the next mile through the thick brush of the woods was much slower.

Isaiah was amazed at the determination of the young man. Gary was well past the point of blacking out from the alcohol, and his heart was likely exploding in his chest trying to keep up with the mix of adrenaline and booze flowing through his veins.

The boy kept going through the thick brush, powering through while the branches and vines cut at his exposed arms and tore at his jeans.

Finally, as Gary came upon a trail in the woods, he slowed, dropped to one knee, and fell face-first onto the sandy path.

Isaiah was only seconds behind. He found the boy and thanked the Lord that Gary was still breathing as Isaiah saw sand flick up and away from the boy's mouth at regular intervals. The young athletic body finally had had enough. It shut down.

Isaiah sat next to Gary and looked around. A few stars shone through the treetops as the trail cut a line in the otherwise pitch-black forest. Isaiah took a deep breath, relieved to finally be done running but now wondering what to do next. He spoke more to himself as he looked to the unconscious boy.

"What happened?" he asked, shaking his head and looking around. "And why are you out here?"

Isaiah felt responsible. Gary was in the youth group; he was in the church. He was such a promising young man, but now he lay passed out, in the middle of the night, miles from home with his face in the dirt.

Isaiah patted Gary on the back as he looked up at the stars. He sat in the quiet of the night, hearing only Gary's deep breath push the sand near his mouth.

He considered sleeping next to Gary but figured lying on a dirt path in the middle of a humid spring night was an easy recipe for a sleepless night.

He could wait for Gary to wake up, and who knew how long that would be? He could leave the boy and come back with help, or he could get Gary out of the woods now and bring him home.

The pastor exhaled a deep breath and brushed the dirt off his hands as he made his decision. He couldn't leave Gary here alone and he wasn't going to wait. He would carry the boy out.

He took a long, deep breath, preparing himself to hoist Gary onto his back. He closed his eyes and turned his head toward the sky as he said a prayer.

"Lord, give me strength to help this boy." He paused and laughed at himself; Gary and he were nearly the same size and he was calling him a boy. "Lord, give me the strength to get this *young man* to safety and to guide him in your ways in the days and years to come."

Isaiah began feeling convicted and full of blame after saying the prayer: Here he was asking God for a relationship with Gary when he already had one for years prior.

If God granted him the chance, what would change this time around?

How could he help Gary when he had no idea what went wrong?

Isaiah began feeling like a fraud. Like he was a false preacher, masquerading as a messenger for God, but in reality, he was simply spinning his wheels within the never-ending churn of humanity.

As he dropped his head, he remembered he was still praying.

He continued.

"Lord, I don't know what happened to Gary, what brought him to this point," he paused and gulped as he turned the prayer on himself, "or what happened to me and how I missed the mark in leading this young man, in leading this church.

"But with your guidance, Lord... With your Will, I will find out. I will learn from it."

Isaiah stood and looked down at Gary. He felt stronger, empowered by the prayer and admission that he was as much at fault as anyone, including Gary, for the missteps of his flock.

He knew he wasn't perfect.

He surely was not Jesus.

But he knew that even if he could never achieve perfection, he would still strive for it. He could do his best to avoid as many situations like Gary's as possible. And, first things first, he would get Gary out of the woods and figure out what happened.

He took another long, slow breath as he picked up his head and squatted next to Gary. He arranged the boy's limbs to pick him up.

As he prepared to lift Gary, he looked straight ahead from his squatted position. He saw the flickering light of a fire in the distance.

There were no campgrounds near here, and as far as he knew, he was not close to anyone's backyard. As he thought about where the fire was burning, he realized he did not know exactly where he was.

The path Gary came across during his drunken stupor wound through the woods and led in the direction of the campfire. Isaiah took a few steps toward the flickering flame and squinted, trying to get a sense of where he was and who was there. He thought he heard voices but couldn't tell through the dense forest if he was fifty, one hundred, or two hundred yards away, or who might be there in the middle of the night.

Isaiah wondered out loud to Gary, "Was that where you were going?"

He turned to look through the thick brush from the way they came. He didn't know exactly where they were but knew the direction and could backtrack enough to get them to the main road. It would be a long journey, through thick woods, carrying Gary.

He then looked down the winding path. If it was a campground or someone's house, he might be able to get a ride home. He also might understand if that was where Gary was going.

He contemplated which path to take.

As he dropped down to Gary, he made his decision. Hoisting the young man on his shoulders in a fireman's carry, he turned and walked down the path toward the fire.

Rebecca watched Gary stumble out of the house, and somehow keeping his balance, sprint down the road. Isaiah startled her as he leaped through their front door in pursuit. In hindsight, she was not surprised to see Isaiah follow. They couldn't let him drive or run down dark roads in his condition.

Rebecca remained silent as she walked to the door and watched the two run off into the darkness. The entire group of adolescents behind her was speechless as they lost sight of the two.

Rebecca slowly closed the door and leaned her back against it. Her eyes were open but didn't register what they took in as her mind was lost in the thought of Isaiah and Gary. Eventually, she blinked and picked her head up to the group.

Their eyes were fixed on her.

She quickly composed herself as she clapped her hands and said in an upbeat voice, "Where were we? The rise and fall of God's people in the Old Testament, right?"

She carried out the rest of the night's youth group in Isaiah's place, including closing the discussion that Isaiah started and into the activity. This week's activity was board games, with *Candy Land*, *Scrabble*, *Yahtzee*, and the newly purchased, which Rebecca was personally excited to play, *The Game of Life*. Rebecca instructed the group to line up and count off by fours, with all the ones going to *Candy Land*, twos to *Scrabble*, threes to *Yahtzee*, and fours to *The Game of Life*. The small groups helped the games go quick and the groups rotated when possible to keep it fresh.

Gary and Isaiah loomed heavily in the back of Rebecca's mind as she organized and led the group. It was over an hour since they left and Isaiah had not returned. She was growing more concerned by the minute and the games were a welcome distraction. Outside of calling the police or driving around to look for them, she didn't know what she could do.

Before calling it a night, Rebecca stepped back and observed the young adults. They seemed so innocent, yet she remembered what it was like to be at that age. Being stuck in between childhood and an adult, the various cliques that formed at school and church groups.

The world also seemed to change around these young men and women. When Rebecca and Isaiah grew up, televisions were extremely rare, but now they were becoming more and more common. When they started the youth group, it seemed the kids mostly talked about their hobbies, whether sports, cooking, cars, or baking, but now the kids talked about the shows they watched. "Did you see this" or "I can't believe they did that" seemed to lead conversations she overheard each week.

She began telling the small groups to clean up and head home as they finished each game. Rebecca noticed two girls that seemed to be talking more privately than normal, in low voices and leaning into each other's ears.

It was Carol and Nancy.

Those three girls are always chattering away, Rebecca thought, but then she paused.

Three? There were only two of them tonight.

Barbara was the third in the close-knit trio and she was not here. Rebecca's mind flashed back to Gary, who seemed to be asking about Barbara through slurred words. She felt foolish, so quick to keep the group going that she didn't even think to talk to the girls about Barbara after Gary's scene.

Rebecca pulled the two girls aside as their game ended.

"Girls, I remembered you usually tell me when one of you will miss youth group or church, but you never mentioned why Barbara isn't here tonight."

The two girls turned and looked at each other, giving away that Barbara was the topic of their back and forth whispers.

"Is everything okay?" Rebecca asked calmly. She had a good relationship with the girls and was surprised they held their silence. She waited for another moment without talking, taking turns looking each girl in the eye.

Finally, Carol spoke up.

"We were surprised to see Gary," she said before quickly adding, "Like that, I mean. We were surprised to see Gary like that."

Rebecca cut through the comment quickly. "Why do you seem surprised to see Gary at all?"

The girls again looked at each other instead of answering and Rebecca interrupted, "Girls, my husband is out there." She pointed to the front door. "He's out there chasing down Gary and trying to help him. If you know something about him or Barbara that could help, then please tell me."

The girls were quiet and Rebecca resisted her impulse of raising her voice.

"Well," Nancy came in, "we were surprised to see Gary because we thought he and Barbara were together tonight."

"Why didn't they come here together? They always ride together."

Carol responded quickly this time, eager to share a piece of gossip. "They aren't going steady anymore."

Rebecca was taken aback. She typically overheard more than she cared to know about the young adults' lives, but she had not heard of the breakup.

"If they are not dating anymore, why are they both missing youth group, yet..."

"He wants to get back together, but Barbara doesn't," Carol interrupted. "She said he keeps trying to date her, but she doesn't like his drinking and would rather hang out with his friends."

Nancy elbowed Carol quickly to cut her off. She had said too much.

Rebecca's mind raced: Barbara was not at youth group, not dating Gary, but still hanging out with his friends?

"See you on Sunday, Mrs. Light," Nancy said as she grabbed Carol's hand and moved them both toward the door. "Our ride is here. Bye!"

The girls quickly left and soon Rebecca was alone in the empty house, sitting next to a stack of board games.

Chapter 5

Broken Glass

Isaiah tried listening to the distant voices as he carried Gary toward the campfire, but they were still too far off. His eyes fixed on the flickering flames and shapes walking around the fire pit. The trail was sandy, more like beach sand than hard dirt he could smoothly walk on, and it narrowed, causing him to turn and dip to avoid hitting himself or Gary with various branches.

He was eager to call out for help as he got closer, to ask one of them to help carry Gary. He worked to get closer but instead paused as he heard loud shouts and glass shattering.

KISH!

KISH!

"WOOOO," a far-off male voice shouted, followed by another *KISH sound.*

Isaiah counted three broken glass sounds. He paused and went to one knee, slowly lowering Gary. A good time to rest while he remained cautious.

Soon after the broken glass, he heard two cars squeal away. He waited another moment as the woods remained silent, then hoisted Gary back up on his shoulders and finished his trek toward the camp.

The fire was struggling to hold on to life as its last few flames flickered softly and clung to life on the embers. Isaiah saw the shards of broken beer bottles scattered in the fire, the leftovers of the sounds he heard through the trees that seemed to be a crude attempt of putting out the fire.

Isaiah set Gary down and took in the area, at first smiling as the clearing reminded him of building forts in the woods as a youngster. The smokey smell of the fire filled his lungs as he stretched his tired muscles that carried Gary through the woods.

The camp was a large circular area of cleared brush within larger trees, roughly fifteen feet in diameter. The glowing fire pit was in the center with lawn chairs encircling and facing the pit while two trails opened off the circle on opposing sides.

Two small tables were on one side of the clearing behind the lawn chairs; one held a new plastic Coleman cooler, while the other held a thin stack of magazines and an ashtray.

Isaiah's initial smile turned into a frown and his perception went from a high-level appreciation of the cleared trees into a realization of what it was being used for.

He opened the cooler; it remained half-filled with beer bottles and an opened bottle of Jack Daniel's whiskey.

The ashtray held numerous cigarette butts and remnants of joints, while the sandy area around the firepit held even more cigarette butts, appearing to be discarded with ease on the sandy floor.

Under the tables were a pile of bottles, mostly beer bottles surrounding a few various liquor brands.

Near the ashtray, Isaiah saw the first word in the title of the short stack of magazines: *Playboy*. He had heard enough of this new magazine to know he didn't need to explore the cover or inside it to know what it held.

Isaiah took a deep breath and looked at Gary.

Someone put time and money into making this area. The tables, chairs, and cooler were all newly purchased. Isaiah figured this must be where Gary was headed, where he was now spending his nights.

The boy was seventeen, less than a year away from the legal drinking age but not mentally ready to handle the toxin.

Six months ago, Isaiah would have chosen him to be the next youth group leader, but now...Isaiah shook his head as he thought of the transition in Gary's young life.

Gary was trading youth group for endless booze, smoke, and pictures of naked women that he'd never meet.

"How did this happen?" Isaiah questioned an unconscious Gary as he sat in the dirt next to him.

One of the brightest and most promising young men in Isaiah's church was lying next to him so drunk that being carried on someone's shoulders for hundreds of yards didn't wake him up.

Isaiah thought that if it could happen to Gary, it could happen to any of the youth group members.

Isaiah hoisted Gary back up and continued on the trail to leave the woods.

He was thankful the dirt was compacted on this part of the trail instead of the loose sugar sand near where he found the trail. The grass and brush were worn away from this part of the trail. It was used frequently to visit the clearing.

After another long stretch of trail, Isaiah could begin to make out street lights. The trail finally broke the thick tree line and opened into a parking lot. Isaiah's eyes were already accustomed to the darkness and he took in the buildings surrounding the parking lot as he set Gary down on the moist, dew-filled grass.

Scanning the area, he turned to look back at the trail. To his surprise, the trail was nearly invisible from this vantage point. The opening had a twist to it that kept it hidden within the tree line and overgrown weeds. The only sign of use was the slight wear of the hardy St. Augustine grass leading up to the entrance.

As he turned his attention back to the parking lot and buildings, it dawned on him where he was.

He was at a school.

The same high school his church used to host Sunday service.

The loud ring of the phone in the kitchen woke up Isaiah the next morning. How he hated that phone. He rolled over and pulled his pillow over his head, not knowing what time it was but feeling soreness in his back and legs.

Rebecca came into the room and rubbed his back.

"How you feeling, babe?"

"Tired," Isaiah said in a muffled sound from under his pillow.

"The Freeds are on the phone. It's Gary calling. I could hear George and Margeret in the background. They are not happy with him, to put it mildly."

"I don't know what I'd do if that was our kid," Isaiah said as he slowly pushed back the covers and rose from the bed. He stood and stretched out his back. The effects of carrying Gary were already setting into his now sore muscles.

Rebecca handed him a cup of coffee and kissed him.

"Thanks, babe," he said as he walked to the kitchen to take the call.

After emerging from the hidden trail, Isaiah found the school's payphone and called Rebecca. She drove Isaiah's Dodge and helped load up Gary, propping him up in the middle of the two-seater truck while Isaiah drove them to the Freeds' house. Isaiah had joked they should have laid him in the bed of the truck for the trip, seeing if rolling back and forth from the turns would wake him.

Gary did eventually begin to wake up as they arrived at the Freeds' house and pulled him out of the truck. He was too groggy to speak and still seemed impacted by the alcohol when George and Margeret Freed rushed out of the house. They were still awake, deep into the night, after Gary never came home.

The next day, as Isaiah picked up the receiver of his phone, he heard Gary apologize in a sheepish voice.

"Hello, Pastor. I'm...I'm sorry, sir," Gary said.

"Gary, I'm happy you're safe, but I want to know what exactly you're sorry for," Isaiah quickly retorted.

The young man was quiet, not sure how to answer.

"I don't remember much, Pastor, but my parents tell me you brought me home. I wanted to say sorry that you had to do that but also thank you that you did."

"What happened, Gary? That's not you."

"I don't know, it just..." Gary paused. "It just happened. I'm sorry and thank you."

"Let's talk in person. We can get..."

"I have to go," Gary said loudly, cutting Isaiah off. "My parents are taking me to school."

Gary hung up the phone before Isaiah could respond.

School? Isaiah thought as he looked at the receiver and remembered it was Thursday. Still a school day. He was in dismay thinking everything that happened the night before had happened on a weeknight.

Rebecca sipped her coffee and looked at Isaiah, interested to hear what was said.

"What'd he say?"

"He apologized, but otherwise, not much. He hung up because he had to go to school."

"I'm glad he didn't hurt himself, and I can't believe you carried him through the woods."

"You're telling me," Isaiah said as he arched his back and stretched out.

"You know, after you left last night, Barbara's friends told me that she and Gary broke up."

"Really?"

"Some boys don't handle breakups well," she said passively.

The comment hung in the air.

Isaiah thought, would Gary really get that drunk after being upset about a breakup? It was certainly possible. Guys have done worse things trying to get a girl or trying to forget one.

Rebecca broke the silence as Isaiah turned toward the bedroom, "You going back to bed?"

Isaiah could have easily slept straight through breakfast and close to lunchtime, but the conversation with Gary and the new information awoke him. His mind was racing.

"No, I'm getting dressed and I'll have a cup of coffee with you," he said as he walked to their bedroom.

Rebecca smiled as Isaiah looked back at her. "And then I'm going to school."

Chapter 6

We Cannot Allow That

Isaiah enjoyed coffee with Rebecca for a moment as his body woke up, but his mind quickly went to the high school. He called the office, but there was no answer, not surprising given the hectic morning routines. Betty, the school's lead administrator, was the only person who ever answered the office phone. She was likely out near the bus drop-off or in the high-traffic hallways helping move the kids along to class.

Isaiah got dressed, kissed Rebecca, and drove to the school. He pulled into a full, yet motionless parking lot near the same place Rebecca picked him and Gary up from not even six hours ago.

The first period of the day was underway and he took the quiet parking lot as an opportunity to see what the trail entrance looked like in the light of day. He walked through the lines of cars, getting as close as he could to where he remembered the entrance. It took him nearly five minutes to find the hidden entrance, answering his question on how the trail remained a secret.

In the front office, Isaiah approached Betty with a warm smile and friendly hello. She was the gatekeeper for anyone who wanted to see the principal and she took her position quite seriously. "Mrs. Betty," as she preferred to be called, was quirky and awkward. Not only was she the lead administrator and secretary to the principal, but she was also the principal's mother.

Mrs. Betty's son, Principal Timothy Clandes, was making a name for himself in the city. He made many improvements to the school in his four years as principal. Their athletic programs and band were now regarded as some of the best in the region, regularly traveling to play games or join competitions against the best in Florida and Georgia.

Mrs. Betty always referred to her son formally as "Principal Clandes," however, he told everyone to call him "Principal Tim." The difference led to many playful conversations between mother and son in the school's office. In Isaiah's mind, they were cute, albeit a bit awkward and weird, yet still cute.

Rebecca did not feel the same way. She thought Mrs. Betty was overprotective and creepy.

Less than a year into Tim being principal, the former school admin left abruptly and Mrs. Betty was hired. Rebecca got along great with the former admin, stopping by to chat and drop off baked goods for the staff. Isaiah and Rebecca were sharing the gymnasium and wanted to ensure a positive relationship with the school staff. However, once Mrs. Betty arrived, Rebecca was not made comfortable. Mrs. Betty gave her only short answers, not interested in talking, along with passive remarks about how Rebecca should wait for the bake sale to bring in food.

"We don't need this, young lady," was Mrs. Betty's typical response, and over time, Rebecca gave in to the hint and stopped coming. Yet that didn't stop her from nudging Isaiah to stop by the school every couple of months.

In contrast to Mrs. Betty's short treatment of Rebecca, Isaiah seemed to be welcomed. Mrs. Betty would raise her hands and tell Isaiah how thankful she was to have a man of God in their lives.

Isaiah received a warm welcome once again as he stepped into the main office area.

"Pastor! How are you? We are so grateful to have you here. How was last Sunday's service? It was all cleaned up after Saturday night's basketball game, right? I can talk to maintenance if you need anything."

"Hello, ma'am, good morning. Of course, it was swell."

Mrs. Betty also had the habit of bringing up maintenance each time she spoke to Isaiah. Principal Tim originally was not a fan of a school that had a church service in it every Sunday. He hinted to Isaiah that he should be looking for another location, that being funded primarily by the state budget and hosting a church service was too much overlap in the separation of church and state. The conversation led to Tim allowing Isaiah's service to remain in the gymnasium, but only if Isaiah agreed to pay for a portion of the school's maintenance's cost.

"We must ensure you have the best service required," the Principal would say during the conversation, although Isaiah had never had an issue with the gym being unclean or with their congregation cleaning up after themselves. The cost was minimal and seemed more a matter of pride for the incoming principal. Isaiah told Rebecca, "Let him have this one" as they discussed the final decision.

Principal Tim was friendly, but Isaiah couldn't help but notice that he was always so smooth, so perfect, so polished. It felt too much like an act in Isaiah's eyes. However, when Isaiah heard rumors that Tim was setting the stage for a political run, it all made sense. Isaiah thought he was putting on an act, and of course he was; he was a politician!

Principal Tim's political pursuits were rapidly coming to fruition. In the past two years, Principal Tim had been elected to the county school board as well as the board of directors of the local Chamber of Commerce, along with now being on the board of two areas businesses. He also acted as the host and facilitator of congressional speeches from either party in the districts in and around the North Florida area, making good use of the large auditorium at his high school.

Isaiah was pleased to see that Mrs. Betty was in a good mood.

"Good, good. Glad it was sufficient for you, young man. You know we are going onto regionals after winning on Saturday?"

"That's great," Isaiah responded. "We usually are up to date with the sports, but since I haven't been seeing Gary as much, I am not as much in the know. I should come out myself and see what a great team you put together here."

"You certainly should! Now, what can I do for you, darling?"

"Well, now that I mention Gary, it's him. I want to talk to your son, er, Principal Clandes about Gary."

"We don't have any appointments with you this morning and the principal is leaving soon for his Chamber meeting."

"Hmm, I hate to be a bother, but I think the boy is in trouble. Five minutes is plenty to ensure the principal and I are on the same page."

"I'm sorry, young man, five minutes for you is five minutes stolen from someone else. Besides, we saw Gary this morning."

"You did?"

"Of course, young man. His dad brought him in this morning, and he was steaming mad, while little Gary looked sick to his stomach. They talked to the principal already."

"Good to hear. I would be indebted to you if you allowed me to do the same. Gary's family goes to our church."

Mrs. Betty raised her eyebrows, taken aback by the question.

"We cannot allow that. He is preparing for the Chamber, *AND* I heard they are no longer attending your church, so with this being a school day, I don't see how you have a say in the matter."

Mrs. Betty was matter-of-fact as she talked down to Isaiah. Always calling him "young man" and using the term "we" to deflect her own decisions.

Isaiah decided not to press the issue, but to find another way.

"Well, thank you for your time, ma'am," Isaiah said politely and began to turn away before remembering the hidden trail outside.

"Oh, one more thing, ma'am. Did you know there was a trail over by the far side of the parking lot?"

"There's a lot of woods out there, young man," Mrs. Betty said, letting a sign of agitation rise in her voice.

"You're right, there are," Isaiah said, nodding, "and this one leads to a clearing that is filled with alcohol, joints, and dirty magazines. I hope the principal is aware, ma'am."

Mrs. Betty's eyes widened. "Oh dear, we cannot be associated with anything like that. I will talk to Principal Clandes."

She turned without saying goodbye and began organizing stacks of papers.

Isaiah returned home, unsure of his next steps. Gaining the principal's help was a dead-end, at least for now. He figured he should wait a day or two before contacting Gary's parents to let their emotions settle.

He would have loved to chat with Rebecca, but she was at the Jobs' house spending time with Jimmy's wife Dixie. Years ago, when the Job children were younger, Rebecca spent the majority of Mondays with Dixie, helping her out with the kids and chatting about whatever event was the latest talk of the community. It helped both of them feel their week was off on the right step. Additionally, Dixie always seemed to be in the know, and Isaiah felt he learned more about his church and community from Dixie and Rebecca than he ever could talking to the men in the church.

As the Job children aged and got into school years, Rebecca and Dixie kept their Monday tradition, and it expanded to other days of the week, like Thursday this week. They used the time to take walks together, repair clothes, plan meals, or brainstorm the next church event. It was their meetings that set the foundation for the majority of holiday service events at the church. A small comment from Dixie and Rebecca would get Jimmy and Isaiah off and running to execute the plan.

Isaiah noticed the get-togethers also helped Rebecca through the trying times of failed pregnancies. Isaiah and Rebecca had tried for years after marriage but without success. In their mid-twenties, they decided to stop actively trying when two miscarriages in two years deeply impacted Rebecca. She felt her sense of purpose fading, not only as a woman but as the wife of a pastor. Now, approaching their thirties, every other couple their age seemed to have at least one child if not two or three. The Jobs, for example, were married very young, just like Isaiah and Rebecca, and now in their early thirties, had three kids, one of them turning thirteen and entering into the Lights' youth group. The weekly get-together with Dixie gave Rebecca a chance to be motherly in helping their kids, and another person, outside of Isaiah, to confide in. Over time, and a lot of prayers, Isaiah saw what he thought were the early signs of depression transition back into a normal Rebecca.

With Rebecca out of the house, Isaiah sat at the kitchen table, staring at the floor. He picked up his head and noticed the family Bible his father, Michael, had given him earlier that week. It seemed to glow and call to him. His eyes fixed on the book as if it were the light at the end of a long, dark tunnel. He stood without thinking and walked to his bedside, picking up the book from the small wooden nightstand.

The same feelings he experienced on the day Michael handed it to him overtook him once again. A strange pain followed by a warm, welcoming sensation.

He opened the pages and flipped through, finding himself in 1 John 5. His eyes were drawn to verse 19: *And we know that we are of God, and the whole world lieth in wickedness.*

He read the verse over a second time, and then a third. He thought of the shifting society they were currently in.

The economic boom the country had experienced after World War II led to massive growth. Consumer items such as televisions and automobiles were becoming more and more popular.

Where is it leading us? he thought.

More kids talking about the latest shows instead of reading books.

More automobiles for young drivers to get away from supervision.

Kids were getting into trouble since the beginning of time, but Isaiah felt this was different, like it was an underlying evil in his immediate area that was undermining religious principles.

Drug use was on the rise.

Advertisements were getting more and more sexual.

Dresses were becoming short skirts.

He could go to the local high school football games and see all of this.

Parents were more and more encouraged by the coolers of beer and being seen by other parents instead of spending time with their children.

He was reminded of the book of Zechariah, when God's people return from their Babylon captivity to a warning from the prophet Zechariah about changing their ways or else their cities and way of life would fall again.

But what could he do? Isaiah dropped his head at the thought.

He led a small church in an obscure North Florida town. What in the world could he do to stop a generation from drifting toward sin?

He closed the Bible and gripped it tight.

The warm sensation flowed through him and his doubt turned to confidence.

He was only one man.

But if he could help one person, then it would be worth it.

The world doesn't change all at once.

As he thought of the cultural shift away from worshipping God, he realized it was gradual and that the climb back toward God might take even longer. He sensed that was what he signed up for when he became a pastor: to lead the climb, to help others up the mountain. He could learn from the gradual shift into sin and help turn the tide.

His resolve strengthened as he gripped the Bible tight.

He didn't notice the glow of the book as he took the Bible from one hand and held it close to his chest with both arms.

He squeezed it tight and took a deep breath.

Putting the Bible back down on the nightstand, he rose with fresh confidence and determination. This city was his flock and the youth were sliding.

His mind retraced his steps on the prior night with Gary, going back to the beginning when Gary burst into his front door.

Gary was looking for Barbara.

Chapter 7

But Barbara Wasn't at Youth Group

Isaiah pulled out their phone book and looked up Barbara's family. Finding "Ash, Robert, and Patricia," he dialed the number. As it rang, he thought about how he hated using the phone. He rarely used it and felt uncomfortable on it, tending to get quiet and never having *a real conversation* because you cannot see the person, as he put it.

Patricia picked up and they exchanged pleasantries. She talked fast and was quite comfortable talking on the phone. After a few moments of listening to Patricia bounce from topic to topic, Isaiah dove into his reason for calling.

"Mrs. Ash, your family has been coming to the church a long time now and I wanted to ask about Barbara."

"Barbara? Oh, she loves the church. I can't believe it's been four years already, but you know she met her two best friends, Carol and Nancy, at the church. They have such sweet families. Good girls, ya know, good girls."

Isaiah looked for his spot to cut in, not wanting to interrupt. "Yes, they are. We saw them at youth group last night and that's actually why I called."

"Oh, I heard you had quite an event there last night."

Isaiah was surprised. How did Patricia hear about it since Barbara was not there and what did she hear? It hadn't been twenty-four hours. Had word already spread that fast?

"What event do you mean, ma'am?" he asked, unsure of what she had heard.

"I just can't believe that boy would burst in there making such a scene. I'm glad he left. It's not appropriate for a boy to try and talk to girls like that at a church event, don't ya think?"

"What exactly did you hear happened last night?"

"That Gary boy interrupting your youth group. He is a nice boy and means well. He calls here asking for Barbara from time to time. They are in the same history class, ya know. Such a nice boy."

Isaiah was surprised. Rebecca told him how Gary and Barbara were going steady but recently broke up. However, Barbara's mom was talking like Gary was merely a boy in her class.

"Ma'am, if you don't mind me asking, who did you hear about last night from?"

"I have coffee with Kathleen most mornings, ya know, Nancy's mother."

Isaiah's mind went to the three girls: Barbara, Nancy, and Carol. They were each junior level at the same school that hosted the Lights' church service. The same school Gary went to. The three girls were inseparable ever since they started high school and were in the same freshmen class.

Patricia continued, "Kathleen heard from Ester, ya know, Carol's mother, and that woman loves to talk and talk and talk. She'll call ya after dark sometimes and just expect to talk your ear off. Well, that's what she did to Kathleen last night. She talked her ear off about everything under the sun, including how Gary burst into your house last night trying to ask Barbara some question. I'm glad he left after you had a talking to him. I hope you straightened that boy out. Such a nice boy but could work on his manners."

"Mrs. Ash," Isaiah said, finally interrupting her, "did you talk to Barbara about this?"

"She was already off to school when I met with Kathleen. But why would I have to tell her?"

Isaiah was confused, and he asked what felt obvious to him, "If Gary was looking for Barbara, wouldn't you tell her?"

"Now why on Earth would I have to tell her? How could she miss it, Pastor? She was there. And such a commotion; no wonder she got home so late."

Isaiah realized that Barbara had lied to her parents, telling them she was at youth group. Gary came there looking for her. And when he didn't find her, he turned and ran toward the woods. He was trying to find her.

Isaiah did not want to break the news to Patricia that her daughter was lying to her, but felt he had to. Maybe she could help the situation. He decided to blurt it out.

"Ma'am, Barbara wasn't here last night."

"Oh, Pastor, sometimes we all drift in church and our minds aren't there. Those kids probably do the same every Wednesday," she said dismissively, "I mean, take no offense, but just last week, your message was...rather dull, ya know, and I couldn't..."

"No, no," Isaiah interrupted, trying not to get agitated by the passive insult. "Mrs. Ash, I mean she physically wasn't here last night. Barbara was not at youth group. Carol and Nancy were, but not Barbara. In fact, the reason Gary left so quickly was because she wasn't here."

For the first time in the conversation, Isaiah could tell Patricia was at a loss for words, but it did not last long.

"Pastor, I don't know what kind of trick you're playing or what you're getting at, but I have things to do. I can't listen to you making jokes when I need to get on with things."

Her voice slightly trembled as she finished her comment as if there were a tiny crack in her confident rebuttal.

"Mrs. Ash, I'm serious. I called to ask why she wasn't here and if she's okay."

"You stop it, NOW, this is NOT very pastorly of you," Patricia said as her frustration bubbled over. "Goodbye."

She hung up the phone before Isaiah could get in another word.

Rebecca returned home after lunch to find Isaiah doodling on a notepad at the kitchen table.

He looked up excitedly, "Hey, babe, we have to talk."

"We sure do," she said as she put down her purse and keys, then moved over to kiss her husband.

"I called the Ash family and talked to Patricia," he blurted out.

"You called someone on the phone?" she asked, her voice rising in surprise. "Okay, you go first, but first, tell me what happened at the school," she said as she relented her news to his enthusiasm.

"Well, not much at the school." His eagerness waned. "Mrs. Betty wouldn't let me near Tim."

"What else is new," Rebecca interjected.

Isaiah nodded and continued, "Saying he had some Chamber of Commerce meeting. But I did find out that Paul brought in Gary and talked with the principal right before I got there."

"Ugh." Rebecca sighed, still thinking of Mrs. Betty, " Betty...That lady isn't right. She comes off so nice, but something is off with her."

"She's just trying to support her son. All good assistants are the filters for their boss."

Rebecca mockingly rolled her eyes but didn't disagree.

"Not much going on at the school, but when I got home, I called the Ash family and talked to Patricia."

"Yeah? How'd it go?" Rebecca said curiously.

"I called to ask about Barbara, wondering why Gary was looking for her, and simply to see why Barbara wasn't here last night. She sounded like she had no idea that Gary and Barbara were ever going steady, let alone know they had separated."

"Doesn't surprise me," Rebecca said.

"What do you mean?"

"Patricia is nice, and means well, but she usually cares about talking so much that she never listens. It doesn't surprise me that she doesn't know what is happening, even in her own house. She dominates every conversation."

"Yeah, there was a bit of that today," Isaiah said mildly. "The biggest piece though, and why she hung up on me …"

"She hung up on you?" Rebecca asked in shock.

"You got it. Right after I told her Barbara wasn't here last night. She was insistent that Barbara was and didn't want to hear it otherwise."

Rebecca gave a slight laugh and shook her head.

"What?" Isaiah asked.

"Dixie said Patricia was out of it."

"Dixie? You two talked about this today?"

"How could we talk about anything else? Dixie knows more about this city than anyone."

"What'd she have to say?" Isaiah asked.

"Not much at first. She didn't know Gary came by drunk as a skunk and then ran off. But after I told her what happened, and how Carol and Nancy let it slip that Gary and Barbara broke up, she got on the phone right away and scheduled a lunch.

"She called Ester first thing and invited her over for lunch. Those girls have not been telling their parents everything."

"Wow," Isaiah said, surprised. Those three girls were all kind, helpful, and involved at the church. He wouldn't have believed this if he wasn't hearing it from his wife.

He sat forward in his seat and waited for the rest of what Rebecca had to say.

"Well, except for Carol. She tells her mom everything, and Carol loves talking to Dixie."

Chapter 8

Stakeout

Isaiah decided to stake out the trail leading to the party clearing. He wanted to know if Gary would return and any of the others he saw from a distance the night before.

Jimmy joined Isaiah at Rebecca's request. Rebecca saw how Isaiah's sleepless night was beginning to wear on him as Thursday came to a close.

Isaiah welcomed his friend's company and also admitted that sitting in a quiet car as the sun went down was an easy recipe for him to drift off to sleep.

Isaiah picked up Jimmy and arrived at the school before sundown. Spring league football practice was wrapping up with a few stragglers still chatting in the parking lot. There were a couple of assistant coaches and players chatting as they picked up the remaining balls and cones used in the helmet-only practice. There were also over a dozen locals and former players talking with players as they gathered up their lawn chairs and coolers. This core group of dedicated fans and former players seemed to grow each year as the team's record improved, however,

their growth appeared to hit a road bump with last season's underperformance. Isaiah remembered this time
last year there were at least three to four times as many
people watching the spring practices, most of them trying
to get a view of the new quarterback, Gary Freed.

A group of young men seemed to stare down Isaiah
as he pulled into the parking lot. Isaiah looked back and
noticed Principal Timothy Clandes walking away from the
group with his mother, Mrs. Betty, closely behind.

Isaiah quickly parked and hopped out of the car. He
was not going to miss his chance to talk to the principal
again. In a brisk walk that was nearly a jog, he met the
principal just as he was backing out of his parking space.

"Principal! Principal! Hey there, Tim," Isaiah hollered
as he approached, getting louder as he noticed Principal
Tim was still backing out.

"You're a little late to watch practice," Tim shouted back
as he put the car in drive and began to pull away.

"A word, if you have a moment?"

"Good to see you, Pastor, but it's been a long day and
we still haven't eaten dinner."

Isaiah could tell the principal was trying to leave, so he
rushed into the reason for the conversation.

"It's about Gary. And Barbara. I'm worried about them
and the habits of this generation," he shouted toward the
car.

Tim raised his eyebrows and glanced at his mother in
the passenger seat. "The habits of this generation?"

He turned to Isaiah, who was now at his window, "The habits of this generation? Excuse me, Pastor, but are you saying I can't control my students?"

"No. Not at all," Isaiah replied, not expecting the defensive response.

"You worry about your flock and I'll worry about mine. How's that?"

The principal was bitter and short, out of character from all the other interactions Isaiah previously had with him.

Isaiah ignored the attitude and pushed forward with his conversation.

"We can work together to improve the community. Your school and my church can flourish if we work together. We can both mentor and help kids that are sliding off the path, like Gary, and maybe even Barbara as well with women mentors for girls."

Tim began to roll his eyes but stopped when Mrs. Betty softly touched his arm. The touch seemed to stop Tim from further frustration, and it reminded Isaiah of a mother calming a frustrated toddler.

"Look, I know you only want what's best, but sometimes kids need to find their own way," Tim said in a calm, smooth voice as he smiled. "They crave independence and we have to be there, ready to help guide it a healthy way."

This was the Principal Clandes Isaiah knew, the politician.

Isaiah responded, "Well said, Principal. Take Gary for example, he's such a great kid, but don't you think showing up to youth group, to a pastor's house, as drunk as he was, is a call for help? We are the leaders in this community. We can help set an example for others."

"I agree. That's why I have been mentoring Gary myself for months."

"You have?" Isaiah asked in disbelief.

"Yes, Pastor. You have a good idea; you're just late." Tim paused as he looked at his mother one more time. "And I'll tell you what," he said, turning back to Isaiah. "We'll keep an eye out for Barbara as well. Mrs. Betty knows her and she will keep me posted."

"I appreciate that, but about Gary..."

Tim put his hand up, stopping Isaiah mid-sentence. "I'll handle Gary. Thank you for your concern, Pastor."

Jimmy now arrived behind Isaiah and gave Tim and Mrs. Betty a respectful smile and nod. Mrs. Betty didn't respond while Tim returned the nod as he spoke.

"Now, if you don't mind, it's been a long day for Mom and me. It's time we get dinner and some rest. If you're still concerned with Gary, tell him to get some sleep if he wants to make the team next year," Tim said with a chuckle. "Goodbye, gentlemen."

Tim and Mrs. Betty pulled away as the last few straggling players and fans were also pulling out.

Soon Isaiah and Jimmy were the only ones in the parking lot.

Isaiah's plan was to stake out the trail entrance and see who pulled up. He figured Gary was likely at home sleeping after last night's activities, but he thought the others might show up again. If a group was going to show up on a Wednesday night, drinking around the fire and smashing bottles, why not again the next night?

Jimmy sat quietly in the front seat of Isaiah's pickup, appearing to be in deep thought. With Jimmy's quiet nature, it was normal for him to go long stretches without talking and Isaiah was comfortable with it.

Isaiah's mind raced after talking with Tim, but as the sun set, the dark parking lot weighed his eyelids down. He was losing the fight against the urge to sleep when Jimmy's voice startled him.

"Why does he care about Gary making the team?"

"What? Why does who care?" Isaiah asked as his mind wanted to stay asleep.

"Principal Tim. Why does he care about Gary making the team? Why is it even a question if Gary will make the team? That boy is good and wasn't the reason for their bad season last year. They need some help with their play calling, way too predictable. But Gary is one of the best they got."

Isaiah blinked repeatedly, coming back from his grogginess.

"Tim just wants what's best for the team, and he likes Gary. You remember how much he talked him up last year. But wait, where did this scouting report come from?"

"James Junior wants to try out next year and I want to learn the team. I watched every home game last year and will watch the away games too this year. And if they want to get any better, they have to stop being so predictable. If I know what's coming next, you can darn well bet the other teams sure do too. Gary never stood a chance."

"You ever tell Gary that?"

"I tried to tell his dad, but that man didn't want to hear it. Gary and James Jr. have been friends for years, but they don't talk as much now that Gary started hanging out with the other players and older boys."

"Older boys?"

"Yup," Jimmy said confidently.

"And..." Isaiah said, motioning his hand for Jimmy to go on.

"And, it ain't rocket science: the team had a bad season, Gary put it on his shoulders, now he's spending time with older boys who are eighteen and can buy him beer or the hard stuff."

"He's depressed."

"He's running from it. And if he doesn't face it, he'll be running the rest of his life."

Isaiah nodded in agreement. It felt obvious, but he'd never laid it out as simply as Jimmy did.

"I saw it back when I fought," Jimmy continued. "A good fighter that has a few bad decisions or gets to the end of his career and can't hang 'em up..." He paused, shaking his head and then continued, "Being a punching bag, seen by everyone as the fall guy except yourself, that becomes the norm. If I hadn't met Dixie, I probably would have gone headfirst into that trap. She helped me get out of fighting and eventually into real estate."

They sat quietly for another hour before calling it quits. The parking lot remained just as empty and quiet as it had the previous three hours.

They pulled the car out of the parking lot as Isaiah imagined falling into his comfortable bed next to Rebecca. "I cannot wait to get a good night's sleep."

They pulled out of the parking lot and began to drive home.

"You hear that?" Jimmy interrupted as he held up a finger. "Listen."

Their ears were already adjusted to the silence as they heard a faint sound. It was growing louder as it approached them.

A moment later, lights burst out behind them. Isaiah pulled onto the shoulder as a police car roared past quickly followed by a hearse-style ambulance with a single flashing red light on its roof.

Their path to Jimmy's house led them directly behind the flashing lights, as the car and ambulance that passed them approached two other police cars. Isaiah and Jimmy slowed as they approached the flashing lights.

The lights lit up a crumpled station wagon in the otherwise dark night.

Chapter 9

That's Not from the Crash

As Isaiah and Jimmy pulled up behind the bright flashing lights, they could make out the crumpled station wagon with its front end wrapped around a tree. The ambulance and police cars were surrounding the single-car crash.

This part of the road was well known to be dangerous, with many petitions for extra guard rails on the deceiving turn. The main proponent of the added safety measures was Pete Thompson, who owned a nearby BBQ restaurant. The popular spot was less of a full restaurant and more of an outhouse-sized smoker building surrounded by picnic tables.

The dangerous road had a deceivingly quick bend to the left. By the look of the tire tracks and skid lines, the wagon never saw the turn coming. The tracks showed the car had careened off the road, losing control as its backend fishtailed and the front end impacted a large oak as the car tried to straighten.

Jimmy and Isaiah knew this road and the nearby Pete's BBQ well, eating there frequently and listening to Pete rant about everything from politics to jazz music to religion and of course the road safety of the hard bend near his property.

The restaurant's tables were empty as blue and red lights lashed the still darkness of the night.

Isaiah and Jimmy approached the accident as emergency personnel put two bodies on stretchers and rushed them into the ambulance. It looked to be a man and woman, but they didn't get a look at who the injured people were.

The emergency personnel rushed to retain life in the precious seconds. The unconscious bodies looked lifeless as they were loaded into the long end of the white hearse-style ambulance and doors shut behind them.

Isaiah and Jimmy unintentionally gravitated closer to the scene for a better view before a clean-cut policeman asked them to back up.

"Stay back. Keep room so we can do our job."

"Yes, sir," Isaiah replied quickly. "If there's anything we can do to help, we'll be here."

The cop nodded as he motioned to them to back up further.

Over the next hour, the commotion gradually died down. The ambulance had long since left for the hospital and officers made notes of the crash. Isaiah and Jimmy stayed, feeling drawn to the spot and saying prayers for the victims while feeling mesmerized by the flashing lights and movement in the dark night.

A photographer showed up taking pictures of the tire marks and the damaged wagon. The large flashbulb lit up the night.

A group of officers was radioing for a tow truck and talking in a group within earshot of Isaiah and Jimmy.

"Poor kids, I hope they make it," they overheard one officer say. "Both were unconscious when we got on the scene."

"I recognize the girl. It's the Ash girl."

Isaiah's eyes opened wide. The *Ash* girl.

Barbara.

He looked at the crumpled car again. It had looked familiar to him but hard to place in its damaged state. He realized it now. It was Gary's family's station wagon.

"EXCUSE ME," he shouted to the officer. "Did you say 'Ash'? Was that Barbara Ash in the car?"

"I'm sorry, sir. We cannot disclose that," the officer in charge said sympathetically.

"I know her family, and that looks like the Robert Freed's family station wagon. I am their pastor. Was Gary the other person in the car?"

The head officer walked closer to Isaiah and lowered his voice. "We are not supposed to be talking about victims, but..." The officer seemed to sympathize with Isaiah. "...I'm sorry to tell you, Pastor, but yes, it's Barbara and Gary. Officers are contacting their families now."

"What happened?"

"Lost control. No seat belts. It's bad, Pastor. I recommend you say an extra prayer for them."

"God help them," Isaiah replied.

"Pastor, this might sound like a weird question." The officer got quiet and came in closer to Isaiah, speaking in nearly a whisper. "But these kids are minors and it'll help us understand the situation, and I ask you to keep it only between us."

"Go ahead," Isaiah said curiously.

"Do you know if those two, Gary and Barbara, were involved? Intimately, romantically, I mean."

The question caught Isaiah off guard as he turned to look at Jimmy, who appeared equally surprised.

"They were going steady, but they broke up, or at least I thought they did."

"Really, so they *were* together," the officer said as he turned his head in thought. "Any signs that the boy might have not been happy with her? Or not happy with the breakup and got a little rough with her?"

Isaiah's mind shot back to the prior night when Gary burst through the door of his house in a drunken fit.

"He seemed to be going through a few issues, but he was such a great kid."

"*WAS* a great kid? What changed?"

"He had started spending time with a different crowd, older boys. And drinking."

"Hmmmm," the officer muttered as he jotted down more notes.

"Officer, why do you ask?"

"Do you know if those two were..." he paused for a moment, seemingly embarrassed to say his next words in front of a pastor, "...were they sexually involved? To your knowledge."

"Why do you ask?"

"Well...it's her clothes."

"What about her clothes?"

"She wasn't wearing any."

Chapter 10

How Are They, Doctor?

Isaiah and Rebecca arrived at the hospital early the next morning to find Gary's and Barbara's parents in a quiet waiting room. Each of the four parents looked tired and red-eyed as if they had been crying.

The mothers, Patricia and Frances, sat close together holding hands in an act of mutual reassurance. Patricia held a balled-up tissue and was dabbing the corner of her eye as she saw Rebecca. Rebecca rushed to the women and hugged them both.

"I'm so sorry to hear what happened. How are they doing?"

"Barbara should be out of surgery soon." Patricia sniffed as she spoke, trying to hold back another round of tears as she talked in between pauses of catching her breath. "They had to set her jaw back in place, she's back in surgery now...and she...broke some ribs and her wrist."

Patricia was noticeably less talkative than her usual self. Isaiah saw her shut her eyes tight as she talked to Rebecca, as if willing herself not to see her daughter's injuries in her mind.

Rebecca turned to Gary's mother, Frances, as the shaken mother said, "We saw him last night...and the doctor said they'd let us back soon...His legs..."

Frances paused and sniffed, holding back tears as she began to describe her son's injuries. Her husband, Paul, picked up where Frances stopped and shouted toward Isaiah in a frustrated tone, "They think he shattered a hip and broke both of his legs. He might not walk again."

Paul pressed his lips tight and clenched his fists, raising one like he was going to punch the wall next to him but lowering it before he acted on the impulse. He stood up and began to pace, mirroring what Robert, Barbara's father, was already doing.

"I'm sorry to hear that," Isaiah said sympathetically.

Isaiah told Rebecca about the relationship questions the officer made to him the night before. They agreed to tread lightly with the kids' parents. It was a sensitive subject and clearly an emotional time for everyone.

Silence hung in the air for minutes that felt like hours. The fathers continued pacing, avoiding each other and staying on opposite ends of the room, while the mothers continued to squeeze each other's hands tight, appearing to always be on the verge of tears.

Rebecca eventually broke the silence, and she wished she held her tongue as soon as she let it out. "Any word about *when* we'll hear what's happening?"

Robert jumped at the comment like he was a lit fuse, waiting for a sound to finally reach detonation.

"WHAT'S HAPPENING," he shouted. "WHAT'S HAPPENING? The doctors are trying to fix my daughter's face after their drunk son nearly killed her! That's WHAT'S HAPPENING."

Robert seemed to reignite an earlier argument from before the Lights' arrived.

"OH PLEASE," Paul shouted in return. "Gary said Barbara needed help. That's the only reason he left. You tell me why your daughter was in trouble, what was she doing out of the house? And where were you?"

Paul spoke in an accusation and Robert took an aggressive tone in his response, each man now standing tall and eyeing the other.

"She hasn't talked about Gary in weeks. How does he know what help she needs, HUH?"

A nurse came through the doors in response to the yelling, "EXCUSE ME, this is a hospital. I am going to ask you to leave if you cannot keep your voices down."

She looked around the room, at Robert and Paul, and then continued, "We are doing what we can and the doctor will be out soon."

Both men went back to pacing in their respective corners and the nurse gave them each a cold stare.

Before the nurse could return behind the door, a doctor came out followed by two police officers that stood quietly behind the doctor. The large officers reminded Isaiah of bodyguards as he caught the eye of one of them, who returned a piercing stare. He locked eyes with him and appeared to size him up in an unexpected way, as a boxer might eye his opponent across the ring before the opening bell.

All four parents were now on their feet and looking toward the doctor, hopeful of good news. The doctor was a short man with tan skin, a clean-shaven face, and salt and pepper-colored hair. He first looked toward Barbara's parents.

"She is out of surgery and is stable. She did well and her jaw is set properly, which means it should heal with minimal signs, but we can never be sure of these things. She'll have headgear to wear for three months. I want to warn you that it may look bad. Also, you'll need to help her eat only liquids while the structure is in place, but if, IF, it heals properly, then I am hopeful she will have normal jaw function in four to six months."

"Can we see her?" Patricia asked eagerly.

"Soon." He turned toward the nurse. "Nurse, can you bring the Ash family to my office?"

"Yes, Doctor."

"The nurse will bring you to my office, where these men have a few questions for you. Strictly procedural for these types of incidents with minors." The doctor motioned to the officers behind him, for the first time acknowledging their presence. Robert didn't follow the nurse at first as he gave the officers a skeptical look, but Patricia's eagerness pulled him along.

As the nurse led Robert and Patricia through the doors, one officer followed.

The doctor turned toward the Freeds. "Gary is waking up, which is a wonderful sign. The head trauma he sustained can lead to comas, or worse, but he is waking up. I will take you to see him now. Please remember, with his lower-body injuries, he will need to be immobilized for quite some time and whether he can walk in the future is yet to be determined."

The doctor paused a moment, looking down at his chart and flipping pages.

He looked up and turned to open the door for the Freeds. "Please, follow me."

Isaiah and Rebecca watched as the Freeds followed the doctor through the door. The remaining officer, the same one that had been eyeing Isaiah, now approached him.

"Sir, were you the pastor at the scene of the accident last night?"

"Yes, sir. I was. How can I help?"

"I'd like to ask you some questions on how you know the victim and how you found yourself at the scene of the accident."

"Sure," Isaiah responded.

"You were there rather quickly, wouldn't you say?"

The statement from the officer was direct and accusatory.

"We were driving by, and did you say victim? Don't you mean victims?" Isaiah asked, stressing the plural in *victims*.

"Please clarify your answer, sir. How did you find yourself at the scene of the accident?"

Isaiah wasn't sure where the officer was going with this, and he directly answered the question. "We saw the ambulance and cop cars on our way to Jimmy's, I mean Mr. James Job's, house and we decided to pull over."

"That is unusual for someone to pull over, most people drive by slowly, but not pull over."

"I suppose, but..."

"Where were you coming from when you saw the lights and *decided* to pullover?" The officer cut him off with another question before Isaiah could respond to the prior comment.

"At the high school, sir."

"Why were you at the high school and who were you with?"

The tone of the officer's questioning was becoming more direct, more of an interrogation. Rebecca stepped forward to Isaiah's side and held her husband's hand.

Isaiah turned and smiled in Rebecca's direction.

He could refuse to answer the questions, but he had nothing to hide.

"I was with a friend, as I mentioned we were on the way to his house, Mr. James Job. He was with me because we were concerned with Gary Freed and an area I found in the woods the night before."

"You mean the night before when Gary left your house intoxicated?"

"Yes, but," Isaiah paused, realizing the phrasing of the question, "but he showed up like that. I followed him and helped him home."

"Sir, please place your hands behind your back."

"Excuse me? What is going on here, officer?" Isaiah held his hand up in a stopping motion.

"I won't ask you again."

The officer pulled Isaiah's arm forward and forcefully twisted it into a painful position.

"OFFICER," Isaiah shouted in a confused defense of what was happening.

"You are under arrest."

"What for?"

Isaiah shouted but the officer only strengthened his physical position with each word Isaiah spoke.

Rebecca spoke up, "Sir, help us understand why you are doing this. We are pastors; we want to help."

Her question didn't accelerate his aggression like Isaiah's had, but he only tightened his grip as he brought out his handcuffs and put them on Isaiah.

The officer responded, seemingly out of frustration, to enlighten her of what was obvious to him.

"Ma'am, there are signs of physical and sexual abuse on a female minor, known alcohol abuse by another underage minor, and a near-fatal car crash that could have killed both of them. Your husband," he shoved Isaiah and grabbed ahold of the handcuffs to jerk him back, "your husband was with the perpetrator the night of the incident and the night prior. He admitted to the boy leaving your house intoxicated and also admitted to being with the boy at an area of suspected drug abuse."

He looked directly into Rebecca's eyes as he pushed Isaiah past her.

"Your husband is under arrest."

Chapter 11

Interrogation

I saiah was brought to the police precinct, where he was fingerprinted and put into a small room without windows or clocks. The room smelled of stale air and mildew. With no sense of time, he guessed it was a couple of hours later when Detective Ross entered the room. He had thick black hair and wore slacks and a button-up dress shirt that was tight over his broad shoulders and large chest. His face held a thick black mustache, but was otherwise clean-shaven, and looked through a pair of thin-framed glasses that looked out of place on top of his muscular frame.

Without saying hello or motioning to Isaiah, he sat down and flipped through papers within a file. The man's attention turned to a notepad in his hand that flipped back and forth pages as he studied the writing. He sat down across from Isaiah and did not speak for what seemed like ten minutes as Isaiah sat patiently, resisting the urge to unleash his frustration.

Finally, he spoke. "Hello, I'm Detective Martin Ross. Could you please state your name?"

"Isaiah Light," Isaiah said calmly, successfully hiding his irritation.

"Thank you. How do you know Miss Barbara Ash?"

"Her family attends our church and she has been attending our weekly youth group for the past few years."

"How long has the Ash family attended your church?"

"At least a few years, maybe more."

"Please be specific. And how long has Miss Barbara Ash attended the youth group?"

"Since she was in high school, so coming up on three years now," Isaiah responded.

"So you watched her come of age as a young woman?"

"Excuse me?"

Detective Ross stayed silent, with his eyes fixed on Isaiah's every move. He carefully watched Isaiah's facial reactions, the tone in his voice, and for a glimpse of perspiration on his forehead.

Detective Ross asked his questions as calmly and smoothly as he would have asked someone to pass the sugar. The calm and consistent manner in such a situation began to break down Isaiah's patience.

"What are you getting at?" Isaiah questioned, now actively showing his frustration.

"Miss Ash is an attractive young lady. You surely noticed her becoming a woman as she grew up right in front of you," Detective Ross said in a cool and calm voice.

"She's a child," Isaiah said sternly as he locked eyes with the detective, "and I'm married."

The detective's gaze held firm, unfazed by Isaiah's direct response.

Detective Ross continued, "She is of childbearing age, that is a fact. Now, please answer my question: Do you agree that she is a good-looking young woman?"

"This is not appropriate," Isaiah retaliated. "I want a lawyer."

"Your wife thought so too. She has one on the way, a good one too from what I hear, but funny," Detective Ross made eye contact with Isaiah, "he keeps getting sent to the wrong precinct. Something must be wrong with your booking file; nobody knows exactly where you are being held."

Detective Ross didn't speak for a long moment as he studied Isaiah. His stare was locked on Isaiah's eyes, yet somehow he seemed to look Isaiah up and down from head to toe without a single twitch of his pupil.

He was sizing up Isaiah, determining the best route to proceed with the questioning.

Detective Ross opened his mouth for a split second, but held his tongue, and contemplated his words as he altered the conversation. It was the first change in demeanor that Detective Ross showed during the interrogation.

"Pastor, I have a long list of victims. And I'm going to be honest with you. You are the connection. You have a link to each and every case, just as our tip suggested."

Isaiah was unsure how to react. *"Victims,"* just as the *"tip suggested"*? he thought. He held his mouth tight in a stern flat expression and nodded, neither agreeing nor disagreeing.

Detective Ross continued, "Tell me about Joan Auferetur."

Isaiah was taken aback as he blurted out in surprise, "Joan?"

"Yes. Joan. You were close with her. Even attended both of her funerals, the short service locally and the burial service in Georgia."

"I was her pastor, and we knew her family, her parents, for a long time."

"Were you aware that Joan told her parents she was seeing someone the week before her death?"

"No." Isaiah shrugged.

"Unfortunately, she had not introduced the person to them yet, or even told her mom the man's name. She told her mom it was a public figure and they wanted to keep it quiet. Yet she confided in her mother that she would announce their relationship soon."

Isaiah did not respond. His mind was stuck on the revelation of Joan dating someone right before her death. She told Rebecca everything, but Rebecca had not mentioned or known about the relationship.

Detective Ross continued, "When was the last time you saw Ms. Auferetur alive?"

Isaiah thought for a moment. Part of him wanted to shut down, to no longer answer any questions, however, he was now learning from the detective's questions and wanted to see where this was going. He swallowed his frustration and anger, doing his best to stay calm and directly answer the question.

"Maybe, six months? Six months before she passed," Isaiah answered.

"I find that hard to believe."

Silence hung in the air on the comment before the detective continued.

"I find it hard to believe because Miss Joan's mother said her daughter was frequently coming to this part of town. In fact, she said her daughter was coming over here at least once per week, maybe more often in the month leading to her death. So I repeat, I find it hard to believe that you never saw her in that entire time. She never came by? She never stopped to see your wife, Mrs. Rebecca Light? She never came by to see..." He paused for a moment, tilting his head and staring straight at Isaiah. "To see YOU?"

Isaiah replied, "She used to come by and help at youth group or meet Rebecca for lunch. They were close as Joan went through high school and attended..." Isaiah stopped mid-sentence. He was thinking of answering the first set of questions before listening to the detective's last comment.

It now dawned on him the line of questioning he had asked: "*To see YOU.*"

Isaiah did not respond. Frustration was welling up and the entire situation was building on him, as if he was in a hole and the walls around him were inching higher with every question.

Detective Ross pounced on his silence and took the opportunity to go harder into Isaiah's personal life. "Does it frustrate you to have no children?"

Isaiah was staring into a corner of the room, looking away from the detective when the question came. Isaiah's now watery eyes shifted to peer directly into the detective's eyes. He lowered his eyebrows and leaned forward, incredulous at the pivot in questioning.

"THAT'S NONE OF YOUR BUSINESS!"

He didn't mean to shout, but he yelled it at the stoic detective, who remained motionless, as if expecting the rise in emotion.

"Does your wife know that you are looking at younger women? Is she aware that you are tied to Miss Auferetur and Miss Ash, both young, attractive women whom you've spent time with?"

The detective's cold expression turned into an accusing frown as he continued, "Is she aware of the five other young women's bodies I have that can be linked to you?"

"WHAT?" Isaiah instinctively shouted, but Detective Ross stood up from his chair and spoke boldly down to the pastor.

"Let me guess," the detective said as he raised his volume. "Your wife can't have children, can she? And you were a good husband for years, but now it's your turn; you need your legacy. But you can't leave your wife, not as the head of the church, no no." The detective shook his head as he stepped to the side of the table between them. "So you find young girls, GIRLS, who trust you. GIRLS, who you can take out your emotions on, your anger on. You cry every month with your wife when the next attempt fails, but it's a charade. You take out your real feelings on these innocent girls and then toss them to the side once you're done with them. Do I have it right, PASTOR?"

If Isaiah wasn't handcuffed, he would have punched the detective. He tried to stand up but was held down with the cuffs in the chair behind his back. His eyes were watering and his face was bright red in fury.

Part of the detective's hypothesis was right; they had cried each month for years. They had tried each and every month for a baby, but it was not to be. Years after first trying, they gradually had begun to accept that children were not in their future. Adoption came up, but the subject was still too painful.

The thought of the detective attacking such a personal matter and using it as a motive for horrible crimes set Isaiah's blood on fire. He could still feel Rebecca's trembling body as she cried into the night. The times she needed to be held and the times she was so upset that she refused to be touched.

Isaiah tried shooting up and out of the chair; he saw himself grabbing Detective Ross by the collar and punching him until the man fell backward. But the handcuffs held him down and the skin on his wrists tore against the cool metal. He remained in his seat and tried to regain some semblance of composure.

He said a short prayer to himself. "Lord, be with me," and took in a long breath in and out of his nose. His emotions finally subsided. Before, he felt as if he could have stood up to fight the detective, while a small part of himself wanted to break down in a puddle of tears as he remembered the heartbreak, but his mind regained its composure.

Curiosity at the detective's line of questioning crept to the top of his mind.

"You're wrong," Isaiah said firmly as he looked down at the table in front of him. He forced himself to remain calm as he tried to separate himself from the moment, to be above it and listen to what the detective was getting at. Maybe they were after the same thing, or same person.

"Is that right?" Detective Ross replied coolly.

"Yes," Isaiah replied, leaning forward in his chair once again.

"We have one other suspect in Miss Ash's case, and like you, I think he knows more than he is letting on. I think he is hiding something from me, and from his parents."

Isaiah looked at the detective cautiously, sitting back and scrunching his eyebrows.

"Gary Freed," the detective clarified.

"Gary's in the hospital."

"And I want to know how he got there, and why Miss Ash wasn't wearing any clothes when that car crashed. You were somehow right there at the scene. Right there, nearly as quick as the ambulance." He paused as he looked at Isaiah. "And I don't believe they were fooling around, at least not with the marks the nurses found. Those aren't teenagers fooling around marks; those are from a man, an angry man."

Isaiah remained silent.

Detective Ross continued, "I can keep you here as long as I want. For as long as I need to decide to charge you with these crimes. Or," he stood up and walked away from the table before turning back to Isaiah, "or, you could help us talk to Gary. His parents won't let us near him, but they might let you."

The detective leaned over the table and looked into Isaiah's eyes. "You want to start clearing your name? This is how you start."

Chapter 12

Charcoal Statues

Isaiah was released ten hours after being arrested. Rebecca was outside the station waiting and she rushed to him and hugged him as if he was gone ten years.

At the sight of Rebecca, he momentarily forgot about the task ahead of him. He held her tight and thanked God he was out of custody and she was okay.

Isaiah didn't want to let go of her, but feeling the eyes of others in front of the police station, she pulled him toward the car and offered to drive as she motioned him to the front seat.

"Thank the Lord, are you okay?" She said as they embraced. "They only told the lawyer where you were a half-hour ago. They said you were never charged with anything."

"I'm okay, much better now that I'm out of there," Isaiah said glancing back at the small building.

"Hungry?" she said as they got in the car and she motioned to a brown bag.

"YES," he said excitedly as he pulled out a BBQ sandwich wrapped in tin foil. The brown bag was sitting on top of his Bible and as he noticed the dark green leather backing of the book, his mixed emotions of anger toward Detective Ross and sympathy toward Barbara and Gary subsided as a calm, yet purposeful, feeling overtook him.

"So we have a lawyer now? Can we afford that?" Isaiah asked with raised eyebrows.

Rebecca smiled, "It's Jimmy's friend, and thankfully he works on favors that Jimmy could cash in on."

He stopped unwrapping the large sandwich and put his hand on the Bible as he looked to Rebecca. "Thank you for bringing the food, I haven't eaten since this morning, and for having the Bible."

The tragedy of the situation and the lives impacted fell on Isaiah and he recognized how grateful he was for his wife. "And for being my wife. I love you so much."

"I love you too."

While Isaiah's mind finally found a moment of rest, Rebecca's now shifted from worry to inquisition as she shifted the truck into gear.

"They wouldn't tell me why they arrested you. Only that you were wanted for questioning. What happened?"

Isaiah finished chewing a large bite and took a deep breath before responding, "I'm a suspect in the disappearance or injury of at least seven young women."

"What?" Rebecca looked at him, wide-eyed, before pulling her attention back on the road.

"I don't think they really consider me a suspect; if so, they wouldn't have let me go. They said Gary is their other suspect and want me to talk to him to find out more about last night, like how Barbara got the injuries she did. Honestly, I don't think they consider Gary a real suspect either."

"Neither do I."

Isaiah was surprised by his wife's response and turned to her with raised eyebrows as he continued eating.

"The police wouldn't talk to me. I tried for hours. Once the lawyer kept getting the runaround, I called Dixie and we tried to piece it all together."

"What'd you find out?"

"You know how I told you Barbara and Gary broke up?"

Isaiah nodded.

"Well, it wasn't just Barbara unhappy with Gary; he was unhappy with her. She started hanging out with his football buddies, and not the ones still on the team. I mean older boys that are out of school and working but still stick around to watch every practice."

Isaiah's mind went to the night before, when he pulled into the parking lot as practice finished and the group of super fans stared in his direction.

Rebecca continued, "These men, these *BOYS*," she emphasized *boys*, reflecting their immaturity, "are out of school but still hang around, the Peter Pan type who apparently never grow up." She turned to Isaiah. "And who apparently go out in the woods to drink all night."

Isaiah took it in before responding, "You think Barbara has been out drinking with them?"

"Her mom thinks she was at youth group Wednesday night, and studying at Carol's the night before, and at Nancy's last weekend."

"And, she wasn't..." Isaiah trailed off as Rebecca shook her head in agreement and continued.

"We know she wasn't at our youth group, and she wasn't at her friends' houses the other nights either."

"How did you find all this out?"

She turned and smiled at Isaiah. "Most girls just want someone to listen."

Isaiah fell asleep quickly that night and was in a deep sleep before Rebecca had brushed her teeth.

He dreamt that night, a vivid, lifelike dream. He would have sworn it was real if he hadn't woken up in a pool of sweat.

In his dream, he was in front of his congregation, preaching like a typical Sunday, when all a sudden, a wailing noise arose from the audience.

He continued to speak, attempting to speak over it, but the noise increased and became deafening, painful to his ears. He looked out over his people as he raised his hands to cover his ears. The parents and grandparents in the crowd were making the noise. They cried and wept as their children turned into charcoal-like statues of ash.

As the children's transformation finalized, the awful sound of endless cries began to subside. The parents were not done crying, however, but they were turning into dust: a brown, sand-like dust that began blowing away in the wind. Their moans carried with them, not dying off but now traveling with the winds and echoing across the bleachers. The gymnasium seemed to more than double in size, now feeling more like a huge cavern than Isaiah's Sunday church.

With the parents blown away and their cries following the swirling breeze, Isaiah was left in the giant gymnasium with the charcoal statues of the next generation. He stepped away from the handmade wooden podium that held his Bible and approached the children. Their features were perfectly preserved in the ash as if they were instantaneously burnt in place, with a look of horror remaining in their expression.

He walked through the crowd, now no longer his typical Sunday congregation in the high school gym, but now it was an endless sea of charcoal children, all motionless and looks of horror on every face, each looking toward him in the center of the endless statues.

Isaiah examined the children. He recognized them from youth group, from local areas, and from school. James Jr., Gary, Barbara, Carol, Nancy; all of them in the crowd.

As his face leaned in for a closer look, the ash children began to grow. Their features and limbs washed away into giant stalks as each child grew wider and taller, now rising above Isaiah's height.

Stalks grew out of the growing pillars and sprouted leaves and petals, still as black as the children were and now over ten feet high...twenty feet...still growing.

Isaiah, now shorter than the lowest petal, was like a mouse in a full-grown cornfield, lost and looking up in wonder and horror. The growing black flowers seemed to eat the light and air around them, consuming the land and growing wider, closing Isaiah in.

Isaiah reached up, scrambling to pull himself up and away from being crushed by the growing black death.

In his frantic clawing, a glimmer of light caught his eye through the endless rows of black stalks ahead of him: it a soft warm glow sitting on top of a thin wooden podium. The wood looked like a pathetic toothpick in a redwood forest, but the warm glow grew stronger as it pulsed.

As the giant black flowers closed off Isaiah's view and took the air from his lungs, the pulsing light shot out like a supernova. The light shot through the giant dead flowers and blew the hard charcoal ash to dust. The flash revealed tall, healthy green flowers. In an instant, the light changed the world around Isaiah, where the ash tomb that had been encasing him was now a gorgeous giant forest of colorful flowers. He could feel the sun and shade on his skin, the fresh air filling his lungs, and the wonderful scent of fresh flowers as he breathed deep.

Then, as fast as the flash came and transformed the death into life, he heard Rebecca's voice. "Hey, Hun, visiting hours start soon. It's time...it's time...it's time."

He shot up in a pool of sweat.

Rebecca was already dressed and in the bathroom brushing her teeth. She wiped her mouth and called back to her husband, "Hey, Hun, visiting hours start soon. It's time."

Chapter 13

Pulling the Thread

Rebecca and Isaiah arrived at the hospital fifteen minutes before visiting hours started. Paul and Frances Freed were already in the waiting room.

Both of Gary's parents seemed like milder versions of themselves from the day before. Frances was still sitting calmly, but her fingers twitched and her mouth frowned unconsciously with clear signs of worry. Paul still had a fire in his eye and looked ready to punch the wall, or anything else in his way, but he was no longer pacing and his formerly clenched fist was now resting on Frances' knee in comfort. His index finger tapped on her knee cap rapidly.

"They're going to let us in soon," Frances said anxiously as she saw Rebecca and Isaiah approach. She stood up and hugged Rebecca.

Paul stood and shook Isaiah's hand. "I heard the police had words with you."

"More than a few words. Yes, sir."

"They think Gary hurt her, and not from the, I mean, they think he hurt her before that."

"Have they talked to him about it?" Isaiah asked.

"No, I wouldn't let them. I'm not letting them near him. No way they are going to get him involved in those accusations. He worshiped Barbara and that's just not him." Paul shook his head as he stared off into the corner of the room, his upper lip in a snarl-like position as he kept his anger at bay. "Besides," he continued, " Gary was out of it yesterday. Too many meds to know what was going on. No sense in talking to cops when he wouldn't even remember."

Isaiah nodded in agreement. "I didn't have much of a choice. They cuffed me and brought me to the station."

"WHAT!" Paul exclaimed.

"Spent the whole day in a small room being interrogated," Isaiah took a deep breath, "and you're right about them wanting to talk to Gary. They asked me to find out what I could from him since you won't let them near your son."

Paul stepped back and eyed Isaiah, as if he was seeing whose side Isaiah was on.

Isaiah continued, "I would like to talk to him, to pray with him, but only if that is okay with you."

Isaiah looked into Paul's eyes. "And he's not the only suspect. They think I'm involved too."

Paul didn't know how to respond. He blinked his watery eyes and lifted his head from looking down to looking at the ceiling. "I know you want what's best for him. Not just anyone would have got him out of those woods and home to us. I didn't realize it at the time, but you did a good thing for a lost boy. Thank you for that." Paul put his hand on Isaiah's shoulder and squeezed. "You can pray and talk to him. I don't know what's going on here, especially with Barbara, but my boy hasn't been the same. Not in months. Please help him, Pastor."

Isaiah began nodding his head, but before he could respond, the door to the patient rooms swung open. A nurse announced that visitors might come back, two at a time and only with a nurse escort.

Frances stepped forward quickly, eager to see her son, and Isaiah turned to Paul and put his hand on the father's shoulder, saying, "Take as long as you need. We'll be here when you're done."

An hour and a half later, Paul and Frances came out of the swinging double doors.

Frances was in higher spirits and she looked to Rebecca, "I'm going to go make that boy a proper meal. We'll be back at lunchtime."

"Thank you for waiting," Paul said. He opened his mouth to say more but stopped himself. He shook Isaiah's hand, and as he walked away, turned to the pastor. "And he's ready to talk to you."

Isaiah and Rebecca were led to the patient room and found Gary with his legs up on pulleys and his back raised up in the hospital bed.

"They said the swelling needs to go down before they will operate or put a cast on," Gary said in a dispassionate voice before Isaiah or Rebecca could say hello.

His legs were elevated and wrapped in bandages while his face was showing a shade of purple bruising. The left side of his face was swollen, noticeably raised, behind his temple and up into his hairline. The blood behind the bruises of the impact was pooling under his eye, forming a deep purple color. His left arm was held in a sling and the visible portions around his bicep and forearm were also a deep purple, matching his eye.

Isaiah and Rebecca smiled sympathetically and slowly approached.

"How you doing, son?" Isaiah instinctively said and regretted the unaware comment as soon as it left his lips.

Gary gave a faint smile but didn't answer.

"Dumb question," Isaiah said and took a seat near Gary's bedside.

"How's Barbara?" Gary asked.

Remembering the update from the doctor the prior morning, Rebecca responded, trying to stay positive, "He's hopeful she'll make a full recovery... And she will have to wear headgear for a few months, at least, but the surgery seemed to go well."

Gary shook his head and his eyes watered.

Isaiah wanted to ask how they crashed, what put them at that speed, in that situation, but he held back. The comment from Gary's dad, Paul, hung in his mind: "My boy hasn't been the same. Not in months."

The timeline matched Gary's disinterest in the church and youth group. The young man showed so much promise, so much life. His athletics, school work, church life, and relationships all had declined within the past few months.

Isaiah started the discussion here, taking Gary back to better days and away from the injuries, the recent crash and horrors of the past few days.

"Gary, back when your family was coming to church regularly, did you know I was planning to ask you to take over the youth group? Not right away, but over time, to become a leader within our church?"

The young man turned to look at Isaiah, a surprised and doubtful look across his face questioning the statement.

"Yes, I'm serious," Isaiah said with a smile and slight laugh. "You had such a great attitude. You were always ready to help, to step up and lead, and you were so passionate about Christ." Isaiah stopped and looked at Gary as the young man's head drifted and looked down.

"What happened, son? Months ago, something changed. What happened?"

Gary didn't immediately answer, and Isaiah left the silence in the air as the boy took a deep breath.

"I just...You can't go far in life unless you're successful. And I need to focus my time on things that will help me."

Isaiah looked across the bed to Rebecca. They shared a concerned look.

"And avoiding church, giving up youth group, is going to make you more successful?" Isaiah questioned.

"I have practice, school work, and a network of similar professionals to build. How can I get ahead in life if I'm failing?"

"Son, those don't sound like your words. Since when does a seventeen-year-old worry about a *network of similar professionals?*"

"SINCE...never mind," Gary's frustration subsided as he spoke.

Isaiah could see the boy was frustrated and he pivoted the conversation.

"What are you calling success? For example, what do you see when you see yourself successful?"

"I don't know. Happy, with a wife, a good job to provide so we have money and can have kids."

"Would you say you were happy this time last year?"

"Yes." Gary slowly nodded in agreement.

"You didn't have a lot of money then, and sure, money is great, but it is not a requirement for being happy."

"What woman would want me if I can't provide?" Gary quickly retorted. "Barbara doesn't..." The boy trailed off as he mentioned Barbara.

Rebecca gave a look to Isaiah, showing she would pick up the conversation.

"Gary, having money is not the same as providing. Money is far from the reason I married Isaiah, but he does provide and so does the Lord."

"You two are different; you're pastors."

Isaiah came back in, "That doesn't mean we don't feel the urge to make more money or want to buy things, like a bigger house or another car or a television. But those things don't give us happiness."

"Well, you need money to have kids, and that's what women want, a husband with money who can pay for their kids."

"Oh really," Rebecca said sarcastically. "I didn't realize that's what I wanted all these years. Thank you for letting me know." She put her hand on the side of the bed affectionately, showing she was kidding with the boy.

"You two are different," Gary said, echoing his prior statement, "and you don't have kids."

Isaiah watched Rebecca, wondering how she'd respond to the comment.

Rebecca winced slightly but continued the conversation. "That doesn't mean we don't want kids. We don't have children because God hasn't blessed us with them yet, and that's hard to deal with, but it is not a money decision. I wouldn't be with Isaiah if it was a *money* thing. He provides: spiritually, mentally, physically. But most of all, he loves me. That's all a woman really wants, someone to love her, to listen to her, to be her partner. Money is great, but you only need so much, and it comes and goes, but providing love, loving someone as you love yourself, is *really* providing."

Gary was silent as he contemplated what Rebecca said.

After a moment of silence, Isaiah decided it was time to ask the question that remained on his mind.

"Son, how did you and Barbara crash? How did you get to that point?"

"I never meant for this to happen," Gary said as his eyes watered. "I was just trying to show her I can be mature, hang out with people with jobs, so she knew I could provide."

He paused for a moment, as if he was going to cry but he sniffed and held back the tears as he looked down into his lap.

Rebecca motioned to Isaiah that she would step out, giving them one-to-one privacy.

Moments after she stepped out, Gary resumed talking, "I let everyone down."

"I'm not so sure I would say that," Isaiah responded.

"Oh yeah? My grades stink, Barbara dumped me, we had the worst season ever, and now I nearly killed her trying to save her. I can't do anything right."

The boy was becoming more depressed with every word he spoke. Isaiah wanted to go through his list, to rebuke each statement and show how life can be difficult, and we don't always win, but he couldn't pull Gary from this. The young man had to pull himself up or else he'd be right back in his hole as soon as Isaiah left.

"Gary, you listened to a lot of sermons and messages over the years, right?"

"Yes, sir," Gary said in a soft voice, nearly sobbing.

"Do you remember any person that didn't screw up at some point? I mean, outside of Jesus, was anyone perfect in that book?"

Gary shrugged.

"I'll help you with the easy questions," Isaiah said playfully, nudging the side of the hospital bed. "NO!"

Gary let a slight smile crack but kept his head down as Isaiah continued, "Every single person, storyline, city, you name it: FAILS. Moses watches the Red Sea part but doesn't trust God to let water come from the rock. Aaron gets about two seconds of leadership and the entire community begins worshipping idols. David kills Goliath, becomes king, then commits adultery and sends the husband off to die to cover up his mistakes. Should I continue?"

Without giving a moment for Gary to respond, Isaiah kept going.

"The takeaway from those failures is that the righteous followers realized their sin and turned to God for correction," Isaiah paused, studying Gary for a moment before continuing.

"Let's fast forward all the way to Jesus and the disciples. I won't even state the obvious of Peter denouncing Christ three times, after Jesus TOLD HIM HE WOULD, but how about when Jesus is guiding the disciples, showing them miracle after miracle, then goes up with three of them on the mountain and gets transfigured only to come down to see his disciples failing to cast out a spirit. Jesus is not happy, but you know what he does?"

"What?" Gary was gradually showing more interest, now with his head looking at Isaiah instead of in his lap.

"He loves them anyway. He still teaches them. He still helps them." Isaiah paused, returning his voice to its normal tone and cadence. "And that's true even after Jesus was resurrected, even after he went to heaven. He still loves us, not because we are perfect, but because we are his children.

"Sometimes things fall apart so they can be rebuilt. Maybe this accident isn't a punishment but a chance to center yourself. It's ultimately God's choice to save us, and we don't know why he does what he does, but we can do our best with what he's given us. We can work and pray instead of pray and wait.

"If you're worried about your grades, seems like you have time to study now.

"If you're worried about your play on the field, seems like you have time to dissect the games to see where the team *and you* can improve.

"If you want to be a man that a woman wants, seems like you should start studying Psalms and Song of Solomon to learn from God, *the creator of love*, instead of imagining that money will solve your problems."

Gary gave Isaiah a smile and nodded.

"Can I come to see you again later tonight?"

"Yes." Gary paused and looked up into Isaiah's eyes. "And thank you, Pastor."

Chapter 14

Save Her

Rebecca left Gary's room and started back to the waiting room, but she stopped when a voice caught her attention. She recognized it but couldn't place it.

With no nurses to shoo her out of the halls, she followed the voice deeper down the hall. Finding the source, she peered into the window on the door.

It was Barbara's room.

She was awake and wide-eyed, staring intently at the source of the voice.

Rebecca pivoted her view to see Mrs. Betty. She was not quite scolding the young girl, but whatever she was instructing, she had Barbara's undivided attention as she dictated how the young girl should act. As if Barbara was a young princess in Victorian England and Headmaster Betty was explaining proper manners that a lady must have. From the perceived body language, Rebecca would not have been surprised if Mrs. Betty pulled out a yardstick and slapped Barbara across the head to catch her attention.

Barbara's attention was far from lost on Mrs. Betty. The young girl had headgear and bandages covering her face, unable to speak, but her eyes were intent on Mrs. Betty. The older woman had Barbara's full attention.

"If you put yourself in a compromising situation, there will be consequences!"

Mrs. Betty's voice and tone were becoming forceful. The woman was chopping one hand down on the other in a disciplinary motion.

Rebecca could see Barbara's eyes turn from obedient to fearful.

She opened the door, loudly interrupting Mrs. Betty, "Excuse me, just wanted to say hi to each of you while we were passing through."

Mrs. Betty turned, startled and unhappy with the interruption, as if she was a teacher and Rebecca rudely interrupted her critical lecture.

Rebecca didn't acknowledge Mrs. Betty's expression as she spoke to Barbara. "How are you, Barbara?"

"Well," Mrs. Betty responded in kind. "Being interrupted by a medical professional is one thing, but otherwise, it is certainly quite inappropriate to interrupt our work."

"I don't believe she needs reprimanding at this moment. She likely needs a friend," Rebecca said as she stepped fully into the room.

"You don't know the half of it, dear. You and your husband poke your noses around with these kids as if you are experts. Stick to your Bible stories and leave *real education* to the professionals." Mrs. Betty emphasized *real education* in a matter-of-fact, stuck-up tone, as she tilted her head back and looked down her nose at Rebecca.

"You do have more experience with children." Rebecca decided not to have this argument in front of Barbara. "I simply wanted to check on Barbara. Excuse my interruption."

"It is time for us to be going anyway," Mrs. Betty turned to Barbara. "Please take my words seriously, young lady."

Rebecca sidestepped to allow Mrs. Betty's exit. As the older woman passed, she spoke in a soft tone meant only for Rebecca. "You ladies with the good looks...You never consider the impact of your actions. You, for example, Mrs. Light, could do so much more with your life if you align it properly."

"Excuse me," Rebecca replied, raising her eyebrows in offense to Mrs. Betty's comments. "I don't want whatever you think is *proper alignment*."

"Not yet, but we will see," Mrs. Betty said smugly as she left the room.

Rebecca allowed the door to close and waited a moment, ensuring the woman was indeed leaving. Rebecca turned to Barbara. "Don't you hate it how she uses *we* and *us* instead of talking about herself? If she wasn't so consistently stuck up, I'd swear she had a split personality."

She noticed Barbara trying to hold back a laugh that must have been painful given her condition.

"I'm sorry, I'm sorry." Rebecca smiled and held her palms up as she approached the bed. "I should not talk that way about her."

She pulled a chair next to the head of the bed and gave the young woman a soft smile, resetting the conversation. "How are you, dear?"

Barbara shrugged her shoulders in an "I'm okay" sort of way.

"Do you want to talk about it?"

She shook her head no.

"I know what it's like to be a teenager. Believe it or not, less than ten years ago, I was one...It can be hard for a young woman, especially if you're trying to get a boy to notice you."

Rebecca looked at Barbara, but Barbara looked away.

"You sure you don't want to talk about it?"

Rebecca sat for a moment with Barbara before having an idea.

"Here." Rebecca pulled a small notepad and pencil from her purse. "Let's keep it short and sweet to start. What's on your mind? Write it."

Barbara's eyes scanned the room as they made their way to the notepad. Gazing into the pad as if she was unsure, but eventually took the pad and pencil.

Hovering the pencil in the air for a moment, she eventually began putting her thoughts to paper and tilted it for Rebecca to read.

Rebecca softly read it aloud, as if a secret conversation for only them. "'How is Gary?' He's okay, a lot of bruising, swelling, and damage to his legs and hips, which may be broken, but you two are lucky. The car wasn't so lucky."

Barbara nodded in agreement and took in the notepad, adding more to the paper.

"Tell him I'm sorry?"

"Of course I can tell him. But, sweetie, what are you sorry for?"

Barbara could not move her head but only a few centimeters and she shook it to the extent of her movement, not wanting to explain her reasoning.

She began writing again.

"Tell him thank you."

"Again, yes, I'll tell him. Barbara, have you talked to your parents about this, or to the police. Sometimes young boys can get overly aggressive. If Gary pushed you or forced himself..."

Barbara's head jerked back and forth, a more forceful NO than before.

Back to the pad, she wrote, "Not Gary."

"Barbara, you were found naked in the car crash with marks that don't come from normal romance. What happened?"

Barbara forcefully tapped the pad again. "Not Gary. Not Gary."

"I don't understand," Rebecca continued, trying to get more from the girl. "You were with Gary, so if not Gary, then who?"

The girl settled her shaking body, as if debating her next message.

She looked into Rebecca's eyes and the fearful look that Rebecca saw earlier when she interrupted Mrs. Betty returned. The girl's eyes watered and she softly shook her head no, refusing to respond.

The watery eyes turned to full tears that streamed down Barbara's face.

Rebecca moved closer, as close as she could to the bed, and hugged the girl.

Barbara's body shook and the girl cried uncontrollably.

Chapter 15

A Call is Coming

Isaiah and Rebecca left the hospital and caught each other up on the conversations with Gary and Barbara.

Isaiah led with, "I can't imagine it was only the poor season that led to this depression-like state in Gary. I suppose the breakup with Barbara adds to it, but...something else is going on."

"We have to remember these are teenagers," Rebecca responded. "They are going through changes and figuring out their place. Talking to Barbara...I could see she was confused, but also hurt. Remember how impressionable most kids are at that age."

"I'd love to know what is making such an impression on him. Today was the first time in months that I've seen him smile, a real smile." Isaiah paused as they got into the car and sat down. "At least the bright side of this horrible crash is that he may be understanding what is going on, and may help him realize how he got into this funk."

Rebecca nodded as they pulled out of the hospital parking lot.

"You think Gary hurt her?" Isaiah asked.

"No," Barbara said plainly. "And Barbara was quite firm on it too."

"She said that?"

"Well, she can't exactly talk right now, but we started writing on a notepad and communicating as best we could. She made sure I knew it wasn't Gary."

"Notepad? Smart," Isaiah replied.

They sat quietly for the rest of the drive home. As they parked and walked into the house, Isaiah spoke up. "You know what? I think I have my sermon for tomorrow."

Rebecca looked at him, surprised. "What do you mean? You prepare your sermons weeks in advance."

"Yes, but this one won't leave my mind. It feels like it's planted there for a reason, and I'll save the other one for another time."

They entered the house as Isaiah picked up a notepad and began jotting down thoughts, outlining his new sermon. He hardly used his notes when he preached; his old habit of outlining each message took over and engrained the major points in his mind.

Rebecca was pulling out ingredients from the refrigerator, shaking her head at the lack of help the food was giving her. With the commotion of Isaiah being arrested and visiting the hospital, she didn't do her normal Saturday morning shopping. As she looked over the bare cupboards, trying to figure out what the night's meal would be, the phone rang.

The loud ring startled Isaiah and pulled him out of his sermon notes. He dropped his pencil and picked up the phone.

"Hello?"

"Hello, Mr. Light, this is Principal Timothy Clandes. How is your Saturday going, Pastor?"

Rebecca was looking at Isaiah, wondering who was on the phone, and Isaiah made a pleasantly surprised face as he mouthed Tim's name to let Rebecca know.

"Principal Clandes, we're doing well, just back from the hospital. I'm sure you heard of the accident the other night with Gary and Barbara."

"Yes, unfortunately, I have. And that is what I'm calling about." The principal paused for a moment and Isaiah could hear him taking a deep breath. "I'm afraid you were right to be concerned. You know, the other night, when we saw each other in the parking lot, you asked me about Gary and I was in too much of a hurry to listen. I wanted to say I'm sorry and hear you out. To talk this through together."

"That's nice of you to say, Principal. Those two really are nice kids, but this generation is drifting. I'm concerned. How about you join us for church tomorrow and we have lunch afterward? You know where we meet. It's right in your gymnasium!"

Isaiah heard himself sounding more upbeat than he usually was. He was trying to convince the principal to join Sunday's service but sounded desperate.

"I'm not sure I can do that, Pastor, but how about tonight? Any plans for dinner? I'd like to talk to you privately."

Isaiah turned to Rebecca and mouthed, "Dinner?"

She nodded yes, feeling relieved as to only have to make herself food that night.

"I can do that. Anyplace you have in mind?"

"Pete's BBQ. You know it?"

Isaiah smiled as he agreed and hung up the phone.

He began walking back to the small dining table. He opened his mouth to talk to Rebecca but was interrupted by the phone.

Thinking it was the principal again, Isaiah reached and took it off the wall casually. "Yes, sir, what else?"

"Excuse me? Hello?" A woman's voice echoed through the receiver.

"Oh, I'm sorry, hello. This is Isaiah Light, who am I speaking to?"

"Hello, Mr. Light. This is Ann Meadows of the Police Department. I have Detective Ross on the line for you."

"Oh," Isaiah said as he turned to Rebecca and whispered who was on the line. "Yes, sure. Please, put him through. Thank you."

Noises of a connection transfer clicked and then the steady, firm voice of Detective Ross came on the line.

"Mr. Light?"

"Yes, Detective, it's me. And thank you for calling me this time instead of arresting me."

"Mmhmm," the detective dismissed. "Have you talked to Gary?"

"Yes."

"And?"

"I don't think he would hurt Barbara, and Barbara seemed to be telling us the same thing."

"You spoke with Barbara?" Detective Ross questioned.

"My wife, Rebecca, she did. And it was more through a notepad rather than verbal speaking, but we are confident Gary cares about her, and she cared enough to tell Rebecca."

"Caring for someone doesn't mean you won't hurt them. Most murders and rapes are from...well, from those close to the victim."

Isaiah paused for a moment to take in Detective Ross's comment, thinking of the sin in the world and how even the most well-intentioned people can still hurt those close to them.

"Unfortunately, I don't doubt that, Detective, but I don't see it with Gary."

"Neither do I," the detective said softly in response, almost talking to himself more than Isaiah.

Isaiah didn't speak, surprised at the uncharacteristic candor and the shift away from the unemotional and methodical temperament the detective gave off the day before.

After a brief moment of silence, the detective began again, back in his usual firm and direct voice.

"So who were they with?"

"What do you mean? They were the only two in the crash."

"Before the crash."

"Before the crash..." Isaiah trailed off, thinking of the group of older boys he saw watching practice. Jimmy and Rebecca had both mentioned them. His mind also went back to the questions about how he was at the crash so quick.

"Yes, before the crash," the detective burst into Isaiah's train of thought. "You told the officer on the scene that Gary had started spending time with a group of older men. Tell me more about them."

"I'll have to find out. These men have never been to my church or youth group, but I am seeing Gary tonight before visiting hours end. I'll ask him."

"Be sure you do." The detective's voice reminded Isaiah of the accusing nature Detective Ross had when they were in the interrogation room.

Isaiah rebutted the accusing voice. "Detective, if you say I'm a suspect, then why are you talking to me? Why am I helping you gather information from these, these *kids*, that you aren't allowed to speak to without their parents' consent?"

Isaiah could hear the detective take a deep breath on the other end of the line.

The detective's voice dropped again, similar to the earlier comment when he let his personal opinion slip. "Pastor, I'm sorry for the personal accusations and the way I spoke to you yesterday, but I cannot ignore that you are connected to seven deaths that have no other way of being connected. My boss wants me to drop this, but there is something here, I know it, and God help me, I'm going to find it. Your connection," Detective Ross continued, "makes you a person of interest and a top suspect."

"That doesn't explain why you are telling me that or asking me for help."

"You are officially a suspect, but personally, well," the detective paused before carrying on, "we found another body and it doesn't link to you. Another girl that fits the pattern."

"Lord," Isaiah spoke unconsciously.

"She fits the pattern, but the death was not as clean; the person, or persons, are getting sloppy. We need to catch them and stop this, or else...or else more young women are going to die. And for some forsaken reason," the detective's blunt and gruff tone came back, "I think you can help me."

"I will do my best, and pray for those girls' families."

"I want to know who, where, when; all of it from Gary's new friends. Find out everything you can and tell me in the morning."

"In the morning?" Isaiah questioned.

"Yes. Your service still at the high school?"

"Yes!"

"See you there."

Before they hung up, Isaiah began thinking out loud.

"And speaking of high school, I'll talk to Principal Clandes as well. We are going to meet tonight and talk about Gary."

"Timothy Clandes?"

"Yes, sir. He seems to know those men and has a re-lationship with Gary, he's been mentoring him for a long time."

"Hmm," the detective muttered.

"What?"

"How close are you with Mr. Clandes?"

"Not very; we only really talk when matters of using the school's gymnasium come up. But I asked Tim about Gary and he wants to help," Isaiah said in an upbeat tone.

"Mr. Light, when you were arrested, it was because we were tipped off that you had a '*too close*' type of connection to two of the victims. We figured out the rest but never would have unless we first got that tip."

"Who would send you a tip like that about me?"

"The letter we received had a logo and letterhead on it: *From The Office of Principal Timothy Clandes*."

Chapter 16

From The Night of the Crash

Isaiah approached the hospital to see Jimmy and his son James Jr. walking out. They smiled at each other, pleasantly surprised.

Isaiah called out, "Hey, what are you doing here?"

"James here," Jimmy responded, "wanted to see how his buddy was doing and pray over him."

"Good man!" Isaiah exclaimed as he turned to shake James' hand with a smile. "I'm here for the same thing."

"We won't keep you, Pastor," Jimmy said. "Visiting hours end in forty-five minutes."

"Thank you. See you two in the morning," Isaiah responded as he walked past.

Jimmy and James both nodded and waved as Isaiah smiled and turned away, heading into the hospital.

Isaiah entered Gary's room and saw him reading a small book he recognized as a young men's devotional.

He gave it to James Jr. a couple of years ago as a Christmas present and now was pleased to see it being passed on.

Seeing the book made Isaiah wish he had brought his Bible. The version his father, Michael, gave him earlier in the week. It was only a few days ago, but with all the events of the week, it could have been a year ago.

Gary was deep into reading and didn't notice Isaiah come in.

"That's one of my favorite devotionals," Isaiah said calmly as he took the chair next to Gary's bed.

Gary jerked his head up, surprised, and then winced. His movement shook the bed and pulleys that supported his broken lower body, and the young man's face showed the pain.

"Sorry, sorry," Isaiah whispered, holding out his hands in a stopping gesture.

Gary took a moment to settle and then smiled at the pastor. "It's okay, my fault, and I suppose I'm getting used to it. Thanks for coming by again. How are you, Pastor?"

Gary seemed night and day different from the depressed young man he was earlier this week, and even that same morning.

"I'm well, son," Isaiah responded as he was still looking over Gary's legs, then bringing his eyes to meet Gary's. "We don't have much time until one of these nurses is going to shoo me away, so you mind if we get right to it?"

Gary nodded, agreeing.

"Who are those young men you had been hanging out with, the group that hangs out in the clearing in the woods?"

Gary didn't immediately respond, but his expression of surprise and guilt gave away his answer before he said it. He broke eye contact with Isaiah and stared blankly at the wall, as if thinking of how to respond. His blank expression went from empty to sad and his eyes became more watery the more he thought.

Isaiah didn't speak, letting the boy work through his thoughts.

Gary swallowed and seemed to push the sadness down as he clenched his jaw. His sad expression was turning to anger, but before it overtook him, he took a deep breath through his nose and closed his eyes.

As Gary went through his thoughts, Isaiah couldn't help but notice the discolored and swollen face. The bruising and swelling overtook one side of Gary's face, and depending on the way he turned his head, the young man could look nearly normal or like he had just been to hell and back, with the side of his face taking every blow the enemy could give.

"I can't tell you everything, Pastor. It wouldn't be good for you and Rebecca," he said as he looked down over his injuries.

"What do you mean, Rebecca and me?"

Gary ignored the comment and continued, "Those guys are my friends: Craig, Lenny, Vince," he paused, "*were* my friends. We all played together my freshman year; they were seniors. Now they all have jobs and are living on their own."

As Gary spoke about jobs, Isaiah could see the reasoning from the earlier conversation. Gary looked up to these men, and for some reason thought their jobs, their money, their whatever was what he needed himself.

"After last season...well, last season was bad. But a couple of them reached out, said it was okay, they had bad years too. We started going on car rides or out to dinner together, normal stuff, and I thought Barbara would like seeing me with older guys, seeing that I wasn't just some failure."

Gary took a deep breath. "And things were going well, for a little while...but she said we were drinking too much, but then she started doing it too. I mean, she was the first one to suggest liquor over beer, but then she said she didn't like it. She stopped joining us on our rides. And when I still went out with them, she said she didn't want to date me anymore."

The sadness Gary showed a moment ago now returned; he sniffed, holding back the tears from his watery eyes.

"But then she started hanging out with them without me. She said she was over high school and ready for college and a job."

Gary paused for a moment, letting out a breath that seemed forced by frustration. "And she was there the other night."

"What night?" Isaiah questioned.

"Last week, then again this week, then the...the night we crashed."

Isaiah noticed Gary's hands clenched tight. They were squeezing the sheets so hard that Isaiah was surprised the boy wasn't drawing blood from his own fingernails.

Gary's voice took an angry, defensive tone. "I don't know why she thought they could help her find a college. They didn't even go to college, but someone told her they knew people who did, that they could connect them during senior year, that the best colleges want more than just grades; they want social women.

"But it was a lie. I was with Craig on Wednesday, and he told me it was a setup."

"The same Wednesday you came to youth group and ran into the woods?"

"I'm sorry for that, Pastor." Gary put his hands down as he continued his confession. "Sometimes we drank after practice. Craig and I would go back into the clearing and...well, sometimes we got carried away." He slowed his speech down and kept his head down in shame.

Gary then picked his head up and began to talk much faster. "But he told me it...he told me! He said it was all her idea, to get Barbara out and see how far she'd go with the late nights and alcohol."

"Her idea?"

Gary was talking too fast and didn't respond to Isaiah's question. "He said they wanted to get Barbara ready for them, that they get taken care of when they help with these sorts of things. That they did it for others recently too, like an older girl they all knew from the swim team."

Isaiah felt goosebumps ride across his body as he listened.

"What girl from the swim team?" Isaiah asked as he grabbed Gary's arm and tightly squeezed it to get the young man's attention.

Gary blinked, coming out of his fast-paced talk. "What?"

"The girl from the swim team, what was her name?"

"I don't...Joe, Joe-Ann." He thought as Isaiah pierced him with his stare. Isaiah held Gary's arm firmly but stayed quiet. He waited for what he knew was coming.

"Joe-Ann, Joe, JOAN! Joan."

Isaiah pulled back. It was Joan. The upbeat young lady he knew years ago from youth group and earlier in Georgia. The young woman who was mysteriously found dead, having been allegedly lost on a hike. She was connected to Gary and Barbara. Connected to this group of men that Gary had been spending time with.

Detective Ross was right, Isaiah was connected.

Isaiah realized that Gary didn't finish his story.

He looked at Gary, "How did you crash?"

Gary shook his head no, not wanting to say.

"Gary, how did you crash?" Isaiah asked again, holding the same firm, direct voice. Isaiah had been involved, and he realized he had responsibility. His flock was being attacked. Whether he liked it or not, he was now more involved than he ever thought he would be.

He felt he now had a duty, a responsibility to find out more.

He asked again as Gary started to comply.

"How did you crash?"

Gary took a deep breath and began, "Barbara was with them. Right after practice, it all happened so quickly. I went to our normal spot, but this time was going to tell them I couldn't be there that night. My dad was hot because of me being out the night before, so I needed to get home straight from practice. But there she was, already with them when I showed up."

Isaiah looked at the young man as he continued.

"They didn't seem drunk, but they were NOT themselves. As if something else had them. When they saw me, it was like an engine started. They all got up and centered around Barbara. They asked if I wanted to go first."

Gary's face resembled a mix of sadness and rage as a bright-eyed fury overtook the unbruised part of his face while his eyes began to water again.

"When I asked what they meant, one of them shoved Barbara to the ground, but held her shirt, ripping it halfway off. She screamed, but they didn't seem to hear...or care. I told them to stop, but Craig laughed. He was my closest friend of the group, but he wasn't himself; none of them were. They were wolves over wounded prey. I pushed someone as they stood over her, but then Craig tackled me and held me down. He said if I wasn't going first, then I would have to watch. That I would watch them all. I was on my back and he pushed my face in the dirt as I saw two of them tear at her clothes."

Gary's rage-filled face grew redder as a tear streamed down from both eyes. He stared at the wall and talked slowly as if seeing a movie of the moment in his mind and describing it in slow motion.

"She was lying on the dirt, kicking at them, screaming, but she couldn't stop them. They held her down, she yelled and clawed at them, but they hit her back, kept her down, and ripped off her clothes. They tore at her, grabbing her legs and forcing her into position. Then..."

Isaiah's eyes watered as he listened to Gary, feeling the young man's sadness and rage for having witnessed this horror.

"Then, I don't know how, but I got free." Gary's head perked up as he seemed to sit up in his hospital bed.

"Somehow, I knocked Craig off me, then charged the two on Barbara with my shoulder. I was the first one to my feet, and I took her hand and we ran. We ran as fast as we could."

Gary's breathing rapidly increased, as if he was running at that very moment.

"We made it to my car and pulled away. They were right behind us, but I...I went faster. I didn't think that car could go that fast, but then..." Gary stopped abruptly, slumping his posture back down in a guilty pose.

"The last thing I remember was flying off the road, the crashing noise was all at once, like a brick to my head. I tried looking at Barbara, but the glass, the trees...I woke up here."

They were both quiet as Gary caught his breath.

Isaiah then leaned in and held Gary's arm. "You saved her, Gary. You're a hero. You have a lot to do to get yourself right, but you're a hero. Please don't ever forget that."

Gary gave a half-smile and nodded.

Isaiah could see the nurses moving about more, and other visitors leaving the rooms. He was getting ready to say goodbye when he remembered something Gary said.

"Gary, you said, '*It was her idea.*' Whose idea?"

Gary didn't answer but looked down and away.

Isaiah was confused by the silence. "You can tell me. Who was it?"

"No. No, Pastor, I can't. She has a way of...of messing with people."

"Gary, yesterday, I left here in a cop car as a suspect for multiple murders. They mentioned Joan, just like you did. I knew her, and I'm already involved."

"Pastor..." Gary looked up at Isaiah, shaking his head no, not wanting to say.

"It's okay, go ahead."

"Mrs. Betty."

Chapter 17

Rebecca's Defense

After Isaiah left, Rebecca felt less obligated to make a normal dinner. She planned to go to the store tomorrow and make a nice lunch and dinner, but tonight, it was only her and whatever she could scrape together.

She took stock of what she had on hand: a tomato, six eggs, a cucumber, two bratwursts, a bag of chips, and half a block of cheddar cheese. She could use one bratwurst with eggs for breakfast in the morning before church, leaving her the vegetables, cheese, at least two of the eggs, and the last bratwurst.

She began boiling a pot of water for hard-boiled eggs and diced the vegetables as she snacked on the chips. She thought the eggs and bratwurst chopped up with the vegetables with a sprinkle of cheese would be an excellent solution, a make-shift cobb salad. Maybe even toss it in some olive oil for a Greek salad style. She was proud of her idea as she ate the chips and set a pot of water on the stove to boil.

Her mind began to drift to her talk with Barbara that morning. She saw in her mind Barbara's eyes grow wide while flashes of the girl vigorously shaking her head within the headgear as she tapped the notepad.

A knock at the door pulled Rebecca out of her thoughts.

She opened the door to find Mrs. Betty, politely smiling and holding a small handbag, just as she had looked at the hospital that morning.

"Hello, Mrs. Light dear, may I come in?"

Surprised, Rebecca responded, "Hello, Mrs. Betty. Sure, come on in."

Mrs. Betty looked around the house and held a disapproving expression on her face as she saw the old hand-me-down furniture and mismatched decor.

Rebecca saw the expression and couldn't imagine what the woman was doing here. She felt herself mentally buckle in for a standoff with the woman.

"How can I help you, Mrs. Betty?"

"Well, dear, is there somewhere we could sit down?"

Rebecca motioned her to the kitchen, where the water was now boiling and the chips were in front of the vegetables.

"Hmm," Mrs. Betty said loudly, as if making sure Rebecca could hear, "I remember when a woman would have a full meal on the table at this time."

Rebecca was expecting to be patient with this woman, but found herself cutting to the point. "Are you here to criticize my meals or for a real reason?"

"Oh, sorry, dear. Please excuse me. A force of habit," Mrs. Betty said, seemingly respecting the direct tone in Rebecca's voice.

The woman sat and continued talking. "My son reminds me to be more polite, but what is polite if not trying to help others by showing them their errors. I think it is drastically impolite to let someone go on, making mistakes without calling them out so they can learn."

"So you're here to correct my mistakes," Rebecca said as she carefully lowered two eggs into the boiling water.

Mrs. Betty took a deep breath and closed her eyes for a moment before speaking. "No, dear. We're here to say: I'm sorry." She said the words as if she was a child being forced by her parents to apologize.

Rebecca raised her eyebrows. "We? And for what exactly are you apologizing for, Mrs. Betty?"

The older woman stared directly at Rebecca, ignoring the "we" question and rolling her eyes but ultimately answering the question. "We're afraid I have been rather rude to you: times when you came into school, and other times, and especially this morning at the hospital."

"That's nice of you to say. And if I've been rude, then I apologize too. Administering a high school cannot be easy."

"No, it is not, but our time is well spent and will not be forever."

"Are you retiring soon?"

"Oh heavens no, dear." Mrs. Betty laughed and waved a hand at Rebecca.

"Would you like something to drink, maybe a glass of tea or water?" Rebecca asked.

"Ice water please, thank you, dear."

Rebecca pulled out a pitcher of ice water from the refrigerator and filled a glass. "If you're not retiring, then what do you mean by *'it won't be forever'?'*

"I suppose there is no harm in telling you." Mrs. Betty leaned in, as if telling a secret, "My Timothy, Principal Clandes, I mean, is going to run for governor next year."

"Wow, that's a big step up for the principal, good for him."

"Yes, very good for us."

Mrs. Betty insisted on always using "we" and "us." It bugged Rebecca, but as the conversation went on, she tried ignoring it.

"And you know, dear, I think he will be an amazing governor." Mrs. Betty nodded her head as if agreeing with her own comments.

"That's sweet of you to say about your son," Rebecca responded.

Mrs. Betty contorted back and gazed at Rebecca. "Excuse me, we are NOT saying that just because he is my son. He will be good at it."

"I didn't mean offense. It's just that he doesn't have any political experience, does he?"

"If he can successfully run a school of hormone-crazed teenagers, we think he can control the governor's responsibilities." She chuckled as if the question was ever in doubt.

Rebecca was silent. The older woman seemed to be in her own world.

"The only issue we can see," Mrs. Betty turned and looked at Rebecca, "is a woman. A wife, to be exact. A strong relationship for all to see."

Rebecca nodded. Even if Mrs. Betty talked in a self-serving manner, she still agreed that marriage was a good thing.

"That'd be great. Principal Clandes would be a great catch for the right woman."

Mrs. Betty continued to look at Rebecca, holding eye contact too long for comfort.

"You know, he is rather brilliant. Any woman would be happy to have him. We've set him up so well, and challenged him, might I add, yet he has exceeded all expectations. I am so proud of him."

"That's nice," Rebecca said passively as she got up to check the eggs on the stove and peek at the bratwurst in the oven.

Mrs. Betty raised her voice, seeming agitated that Rebecca removed her attention from Mrs. Betty's boasting to check on her food.

"You know he does more than anyone will ever see. We've set him up with business relationships from the most influential owners all the way down to key-shift workers. And not only business, but political relationships from congressmen to their administrators. We have made an error, though, and we see that we need to improve our religious relationships."

"You're welcome to come to service tomorrow, and we could always use an extra hand if you want to serve. We'd love to have you." Rebecca was eager to change the subject. She couldn't tell if Mrs. Betty was bragging about her son or herself. All the "we" and "us" usage made Rebecca think Mrs. Betty was the one organizing Principal Clandes' life, and now the woman was openly taking credit for it.

Mrs. Betty didn't acknowledge the invite to service but instead kept talking. "Yes, a religious relationship would be perfect, if even for only a short time. You know, I was originally against it, but after how all those other girls turned out. No, no, no, I couldn't allow those relationships to continue."

"Oh, I didn't realize Principal Clandes had been seeing someone," Rebecca said as she sat back down at the table with Mrs. Betty.

"There's a lot you don't realize, dear."

Rebecca regretted sitting back down; the real Mrs. Betty was coming back out and all her condescending comments came with her.

"If only my Harvey were still here to see this. It's all coming together so perfectly," Mrs. Betty continued as if Rebecca wasn't in the room. The woman gave a long sigh and then perked up and continued speaking, finally getting down to business. "Well, dear, I wanted to excite you with the opportunity you have in front of you. I have no idea why its *you*, but I suppose I can see our reasoning;

you certainly have the looks, background, and no child
ren...that certainly helps for now. But before we finalize
this, I have to know why you do not have children. Is it
you or your husband, the pastor? Do you know?"

Rebecca uncomfortably stood up from her chair and
stepped back. Mrs. Betty stared directly into her eyes
with all seriousness, like it was a simple and straight-
forward question that demanded a quick and honest
response.

"I think it is time for you to leave," Rebecca said coldly.

"Oh dear, are you really that dense? This is the chance
of a lifetime and we're offering you a front-row ticket."

Rebecca didn't respond, returning the eye contact and
standing her ground. The boiling pot of water was the
only sound in the house as the two women held eye
contact.

"We seem to have lost you," Mrs. Betty replied. "We really thought you would jump at this chance, but allow me
to back up. My Timothy controls this city, and to unseeing
eyes that may sound unlikely, but I assure you it's true.
In fact, I make sure it is true by aligning his appointments
and *influencing* anyone who needs it. Now I understand
this may be over your head, being a backwoods religious
homemaker and all, but relationships are a key part of
a rise to power. My Timothy will be governor soon, and
this state will soon be a foothold for his next step into na-
tional power. We need to secure him a wife and religious
base." She motioned her hand to Rebecca.

Rebecca's eyes opened wide. "It's time for you to leave,"
she retorted without breaking eye contact.

Mrs. Betty stood, ignoring the request for a second time.

"Dear, it really is better if you agree. What is it with your generation? They always need convincing. We have done so much yet no one realizes we are inevitable."

Mrs. Betty stepped closer toward Rebecca and to the counter where a pile of diced tomatoes and a large knife waited.

"I'm married, and I'm calling the police. Get out of my house," Rebecca said sternly.

"Dear," Mrs. Betty laughed, "widows make the best story!"

Mrs. Betty's hand extended and she fingered the handle of the nearby knife as she eyed Rebecca. "And the police? Who do you think had them arrest your current husband?" Mrs. Betty asked curiously as she tilted her head.

Rebecca pivoted and grasped the handle of the boiling pot on the stove.

Rebecca was shocked by the consistent look on Mrs. Betty's face. There was no change from the moment she entered the home and made small talk to insinuating that Rebecca was about to be a widow. The old woman was cold, calculated, and by the looks of her hand on the knife, she was also very dangerous.

"Dear, you can agree or not. It doesn't matter in the end, so better to save yourself the trouble. But I do hope you see the bright side. This is an opportunity! And if you don't want it, well," her voice dropped, "there will be consequences. Your husband will be removed no matter

what, that's a fact, dear, but in order to get you onboard-
ed, say...if you need any more convincing...others may
have to suffer until you comply. We are quite good at
removing those who don't agree. It'd be an awful shame
if Barbara and Gary don't make it. They were such a
promising young couple, but too easy in the end. All it
took was pushing the ball in motion and those kids did
the rest themselves. Now, Joan, she put up a fight."

Rebecca's eyes widened and she gripped the handle of
the boiling pot with white knuckles.

Mrs. Betty continued, "But that little harlot eventually got what the rest did as well. We thought we might
have to remove you and your husband before her; you
were poking around way too much, organizing your little
church groups with our students. I mean, come on, dear,
trying to steal our students from us? But now, I like this
better, and you will too."

"GET OUT OF MY HOUSE!"

Rebecca screamed and picked the pot off the stove,
ready to cover Mrs. Betty in boiling water.

As fast as Rebecca picked up the pot, Mrs. Betty had
the knife up and inches away from Rebecca. The old
woman's body was positioned for a stab, but her face was
still as indifferent and unmoved as before. A view of only
her face did not reveal if she was filling out routine office
paperwork or preparing to plunge a knife into the wife of
the local pastor.

"This generation, always needing convincing." Mrs.
Betty shook her head slowly. "We'll be in touch, dear."

With speed and force, Mrs. Betty flicked her wrist and swung the knife down in a swift and forceful motion, driving it into the countertop. Without a change in expression, she turned and calmly walked out of the kitchen and out of the house.

Chapter 18

Black Waves and a Glow

Isaiah arrived at Pete's BBQ and found Principal Clandes waiting at a table with two pulled pork sandwich platters. The crinkle-cut fries gave off steam fresh out of the fryer.

"Perfect timing, Pastor," the principal said. "I hope you don't mind, but I ordered us dinner. Best pulled pork in town."

Isaiah smiled as they greeted with a handshake. "Thank you, Principal. I could smell it as I pulled up, wonderful."

"That smoker is this place's best advertisement. Anyone in a square mile gets hungry. And please, call me Tim."

The two men began eating and making friendly small talk, Tim asking about how the church was going and Isaiah asking about the school and the recent Chamber of Commerce meeting.

The recent conversation with Gary was fresh on Isaiah's mind. He wondered how much the principal knew about the group of recent graduates and how Mrs. Betty was apparently pulling their strings. Isaiah didn't want to jump to conclusions, but the topic had to be discussed. He thought about how to broach the subject as Principal Clandes talked about approvals for large developments downtown and the bright future of the city.

For all Isaiah knew, the principal knew about it all and was allowing it to happen or...or he knew nothing, being so busy with all these other matters. And there was always the possibility that Gary wasn't telling the truth.

Isaiah did consider that Gary could be embellishing or trying to cover his own tracks, but he just couldn't believe that. However, now chatting with the principal, Isaiah seemed to doubt Gary's confession of Mrs. Betty being behind the group of men that were responsible for the murders of multiple women. It seemed so far-fetched now that he listened to Principal Clandes talk about economic development.

How could this man's mother, the stuck up, by-the-book administrator, be involved with these men who were abusing alcohol and doing even worse things to young women? Why? And how many did Detective Ross say? Seven women?

He believed Gary, but did he? Mrs. Betty previously denied knowing about the trail in the woods at school. It simply didn't add up.

After a few more minutes of friendly small talk, Isaiah finally broached the subject.

"On the phone, you mentioned Gary," Isaiah said, nodding to Tim.

"Oh, yes, yes. Well, let me say again, you were right to be concerned and I'm sorry I rushed away the other night. I keep wondering, wishing really, there was some way we could have prevented that horrible crash."

"I came by to see you that morning as well, at the school. But your mother, er, Mrs. Betty said you were busy."

Tim gave a slight laugh. "It's okay to call her my mother. I know it can look a little weird having my mother as my assistant as well as the lead school administrator. It has been nice to be close to her ever since my father passed, and she has been an amazing administrator, and even better mother. But unfortunately, saying no to protect my time is now her default response, even if it impacts people who really need that time. I apologize for that."

"She mentioned that Gary and his father met with you that morning."

"You're right, they did. In fact, I have been talking with Gary twice a month since last fall. I'm not sure if you noticed, but he was quite depressed after last football season. It didn't go as well as we all had hoped. That was an amazing team, but Gary's play just couldn't keep it together, and his friends, grades – all of it seemed to suffer. After that, I sort of took him under my wing, to keep an eye on him and help the boy out."

Isaiah nodded in agreement. "That's good of you, and good to hear. He certainly has not been himself for the past few months. And you know...we should discuss mentoring. Rebecca and I have been considering this for some time, trying to figure out the best way to give one-to-one time in helping young adults. Thankfully for Gary, his father is around and seems involved, but not every kid has that; some need more guidance than what their parents can give."

"That's come up in our staff meetings as well." Tim nodded back. "You know, I feel bad never being involved in your church, especially since we allowed you to move into the gymnasium on Sundays. How are you and the church, and how is the lady of the church, Rebecca?"

"We're doing well. I mean, a pastor's work is never done, so sometimes things can stack up, but every second is from Jesus. We're not on our own clock, but God's, and doing what we can with what he gave us."

Tim coughed and nodded. "I can only imagine." He cleared his throat again. "Excuse me, too big of a bite, too much of it."

Isaiah gave Tim a moment as he cleared his throat and caught his breath.

The principal took a deep breath and returned to normal as he resumed speaking. "Do you mind if I ask a personal question?"

"What is it?" Isaiah responded.

"You and Rebecca seem like you'd be such good parents. How come no children?"

Isaiah's mind flashed away from the conversation, into a vision, a dream. It was only a split second in real time but lasted hours inside Isaiah's mind.

He saw a large dark green leather-bound book, floating in a dark sea, bobbing up and down in the pitch-black waves. As the book came closer into view, he saw it was the Bible his father had recently given him. The inside pages and around the spine were glowing with a soft, warm glow that contrasted with the deep, black water it floated on.

As the book came into view, it rocked violently in the harsh waves, but somehow the book seemed content. Water never washed over it, it never turned, and no matter what the waves did, the Bible rose and fell calmly with the chaos of the pitch-black water.

The image became more clear and Isaiah was now standing at a corner of the Bible, within the warm glow. He peered out over the book that was now immense in his new vantage point. The book was now the size of a football field as he stood in one corner, looking out over the entire sprawling book.

As the giant Bible calmly rocked with the chaotic waves, a haze began to form, like a fog across the surface of the book. Out of the haze, a man stood in front of Isaiah. Isaiah did not recognize the man, but he seemed oddly familiar, like a long-lost relative.

Rebecca now appeared behind Isaiah, gripping his arm at the elbow and pulling herself close, in partnership with Isaiah. She stared at the man from the fog with the same curious familiarity as Isaiah.

The man smiled playfully, with a slight laugh, as if he knew Isaiah, as if he were the first to realize how they knew each other. The man turned to his right, and to Isaiah's surprise, there stood his friend Jimmy.

Jimmy handed the man from the fog a key, placing it neatly in the man's hand.

The moment the man took the key, the black waves erupted underneath the giant floating Bible. Like a geyser, the waves shot up and cried out.

The glow of the book seemed to provide a shield, a forcefield against the splashing waves as the group stood in the corner of the floating book in the black sea.

Nearly as soon as the man took the key from Jimmy, he turned, and with a smile, he handed it to Isaiah.

As Isaiah took the key, the light haze that stretched across the immense book began to thicken. Just as the man first appeared, now an entire group of people stood on top of the giant floating Bible, but they were still in the haze. Not quite fog, but not quite people, as if they were still being formed.

Isaiah looked over the endless sea of people, hidden in the fog, as the black waves splashed around them.

Sometimes the black waves landed on Jimmy or the man in front of Isaiah, and it shook them, turning them back into more haze than man, pulling away their physical being and leaving them a clouded version of themselves. But with every splash that challenged their existence, the glow of the book beneath them replaced their solid structure.

Isaiah looked down at the key, then to Jimmy, who was smiling at Isaiah as he continually transitioned from partial haze to solid structure in the splashing waves and glow.

Jimmy simply smiled and motioned to the man from the fog.

Isaiah then looked to the familiar man. He held up the key for the man to see. It felt bigger than it first felt, and it glowed just like the pages of the giant book they floated on.

"What do I do?" Isaiah asked.

"It's a key, Dad," the man said with a smile, "and it's your turn to use it."

Isaiah mouthed the word *Dad* as he looked at the man.

The man smiled with a soft, friendly laugh, then he pointed to a small hole in the ground at Isaiah's feet.

Isaiah and Rebecca both looked down in unison at the small keyhole. He turned to look at Rebecca. She nodded in agreement and returned her gaze to the keyhole.

Isaiah knelt down and put the key to the hole.

Before he inserted it, he looked back at the man who called him Dad.

"I don't know what this does or who you are, but what...what is all this...what are we doing here?"

Isaiah looked around at the splashing waves and the protective light that kept them at bay.

The man's smile grew even wider and his face beamed like a proud father watching their child take their first steps.

"I'm glad you asked," the man said. "Dad, I won't have much time after you, but that's all relative. Mom comes home first, then you, then me, but ultimately, we are all bricks in a wall. And it's not us who completes this, it's up to them." The man motioned to fog behind him as faces formed and then returned to haze with the splashing water, only to be formed again in the glow of their vessel.

The man from the fog continued, "You start it, I continue it, and they finish it. At least for this stage of the journey. Honestly, it really has no beginning or end that you'd understand right now."

The man smiled as Isaiah was still unsure of what it all meant.

"The next step starts with you, Dad. Right here. It has been hidden for nearly two thousand years, but your next move unleashes it, and unleashes us." He motioned again to the fog as a woman formed at his side, and behind him four grown men, standing tall shoulder-to-shoulder like a wall of muscle. One of the men shone brighter than the others, as if the strength of those next to him was being focused through him.

Children took shape behind the four men. They were at first shielded in the men's shadow before the haze quickly wrapped around them and they grew to adult men and women, some at the four men's sides and some at their back. And yet behind them, a vast array of people began to form, each larger than the ones before them, each glowing bigger and brighter with the glow of the Bible at their feet underneath them. Their feet acted as a conduit for the glow of the book and the glow now encompassed their entire being, shining brighter from the tribe than the book itself.

"We are a people in exile, Father. The culture has shifted so far that it now demands our response. You turn the key to unleash us, you are our leader, you take the wheel and allow us to go forward."

With his last words, *Take the wheel and allow us to go forward,*" the man from the fog, Jimmy, and all the people across the book disappeared.

Isaiah remained knelt down, holding the key with Rebecca at his side. The glowing keyhole at his feet.

The book under their feet began to rock as it tossed in the deep, bottomless black sea. The water splashed the surface and fought with the glow.

The water built up on the book before Isaiah could respond, waves now pushing on him as he held the key in one hand and Rebecca in the other.

He felt Rebecca squeeze his arm tight as the waves overtook them, the book now underwater and their bodies being thrashed by the waves. Yet their feet were still firmly planted, stuck to the surface.

He knelt down, holding the key in the water as the current grew stronger, and pushing against his hand so he couldn't slide it in the keyhole.

The water pushed and pulled on him and grew stronger every second. Rebecca held his arm tight as Isaiah reached forward, holding his breath, holding his wife, and holding a key to unlock the book beneath.

The closer he got to the hole, the stronger the waters pushed.

He felt Rebecca's strong grip fade into a gentle touch as she released, the waters pulling her away.

Now two hands on the key, he steadied himself in the force of the black waters.

The glow of the book was dimming at its edges but brighter under his feet where he contacted it.

In one swift motion, he plunged the key into the hole and turned it.

Instantly, the water subsided like a shadow running from light. The glow of the book became brighter and the sky opened up to a gorgeous blue sky above crystal clear waters.

Rebecca returned at his side, now in a glowing white robe and three times larger than she was before.

The man, Jimmy, and the fog people all reappeared, all larger than life like Rebecca was, and all wearing clothes brighter than the sun and whiter than any shade of white Isaiah could imagine.

Then just as Isaiah felt the presence of his loved ones return, he snapped back to reality.

He was back to sitting at a splintered wooden picnic table with the local principal.

"Are you okay? Isaiah?"

The principal waved his hand in front of Isaiah's face.

Isaiah blinked and shook his head for a moment, gathering himself.

The dream felt so real.

Chapter 19

Not That Simple

Isaiah blinked and took a deep breath, followed by another.

"You okay, Pastor?"

Isaiah looked at the principal, nodding his head, and coming out of his dream with a new perspective.

What was he thinking?

How could he doubt Gary's story?

Sure, it was possible the boy was lying, but it all lined up. A trial in the woods for young men to abuse themselves and others. An overly stubborn and controlling school administrator. A list of women whose lives ended early, and Isaiah as a key connection.

But there was another connection: the school.

Detective Ross mentioned the other women had ties to Isaiah, but if they were in this part of town, they most likely had ties to the high school where his church service was held.

Gary and Barbara were here.

Joan came here to join the swim team.

"Pastor, are you okay?"

Isaiah looked up at the principal. The man was so smooth and easy to talk to that Isaiah had let the topic of Mrs. Betty slip his mind. He came here trying to figure out the truth but found himself agreeing with the man and even about to discuss building a mentoring program with him.

Did Principal Tim know his mother's involvement, the way Gary alluded to it?

Was he aware of the strings his mother was pulling across the town?

This man was either completely oblivious to his mother's actions or he was a part of it.

Isaiah didn't think twice; he let his gut guide him. "How was your mother involved with Gary and Barbara?"

"Excuse me, Pastor," Tim retorted, leaning back in surprise.

"I told her about the trail in the woods and she acted surprised, but after talking with Gary, your mother seemed to know a lot more than she was letting on. How was she involved?"

"Pastor, you just seemed to be in another world and then you come back to life with accusations about my mother?"

"I waited long enough to ask you, and now we need to cover this. I'll ask again. How was your mother involved with Gary and Barbara, let alone the multitude of other women?"

Principal Tim eyed Isaiah, his lip snarled but returned to normal while his eyes flashed with rage at the pastor.

Tim looked down for a moment, then returned to his prior posture and regained eye contact with Isaiah. The rage and snarl were gone, replaced with an understanding and empathic look.

"I'm afraid it's not that simple," Tim said sympathetically.

"NOT THAT SIMPLE?" Isaiah shouted with raised eyebrows in question, not allowing himself to mimic Tim's emotions. "Two kids nearly died, Joan is dead, and from what the police tell me, there have been many others who have died, MURDERED. Your mother, and maybe even you, might be linked to them all. So before I call the police, I'm asking you first: How was your mother involved?"

Principal Clandes again looked down into his lap.

Isaiah could see his shoulders rising and falling and he breathed deep.

Raising his head, Tim said, "My mother is...ill. She has a rare and extreme form of dementia. It's been with her for years, but the past couple years have been much worse. Sometimes she thinks I'm the president, sometimes I'm running a major corporation, or sometimes she can't remember where the refrigerator is. She'll pace the house until nearly collapsing in exhaustion trying to find it, and never have looked in the kitchen."

He paused, turning his head to look at the trees across the parking lot, and then continued.

"She is a good administrator, even with her condition. She doesn't *need* to work at the school for the money, but she does for her health. I ask her to work there to keep her close and because it helps her. The students, the work, the day-to-day; they help her keep her mind straight. At home, it drifts and sometimes she can't remember a thing, but at school...She is back in her old habits and the organization, it just helps. I get extra time with my mother, if only for a fleeting moment, when otherwise her mind is gradually coming to an end."

Isaiah mouthed a response, but no sound left his lips. He wasn't sure how to continue.

Tim continued, "I have slowly watched my mother lose her mind. So I repeat, it's not that simple."

They sat quietly for a moment before the sound of a police siren came into earshot.

It was Detective Ross.

"There is an emergency. You two need to follow me," Detective Ross said before quickly returning to his vehicle and turning around in the dirt lot.

Detective Ross led Isaiah and Tim to a small, tan-colored home that was decorated in an old-fashioned style but with a clean cut and upkept feel. The paint under the windows reminded Isaiah of doilies underneath candy dishes as he approached behind the police cruiser. Principal Tim pulled in quickly behind them, not waiting for Isaiah to fully park.

Three police cars surrounded the dirt driveway as four officers were huddled up in conversation.

Isaiah saw *"Clandes"* in bold black letters on the mailbox, and he turned to see Tim sprinting from his car toward the group of officers.

Detective Ross had led them to Mrs. Betty's house.

Tim rushed to the officers and began shouting questions.

"What are you doing here? Where is my mother? This is madness! You don't know her condition!"

One of the officers responded before Detective Ross was close enough to hear the conversation. "Sir, calm down. You need to back away from the property."

"How dare you!" Tim shouted and Isaiah was surprised at the vengeful tone in his voice. "Do you have any idea…" Principal Timothy paused, catching himself as he raised his finger directly at the young officer's chest. He closed his eyes and took a deep breath and seemed to become a new man, fully composed and pragmatic.

"Officer, that is my mother's house. I need to know if she is okay. She has a condition. And just what are you doing here?"

The officer seemed to disregard Tim's questions. "We received notice of this woman threatening someone, and when we arrived to question her, she threatened us with physical harm."

"Four of you for one old lady, eh?" Detective Ross said as he approached. "Men, I'd like to introduce you to Principal Clandes. He is principal at the local high school."

The officers looked skeptically at the principal as Detective Ross spoke, not impressed by the principal title.

Detective Ross continued, "He also leads the chamber of commerce, numerous local political committees, and sits on the board at two of the largest businesses in town."

The officers' body language changed as they stood up straighter, more at attention and facing Tim. They were now convinced that Timothy Clandes had clout and should be listened to.

"Hello, sir." The officers nodded apologetically toward Tim as they fell in line to listen to Detective Ross, the senior ranking officer on site.

"Really needed four of you and a call to dispatch for this? Give me one moment, please, Mr. Clandes," Detective Ross spoke as he stepped closer to the officers, motioning his index finger to Tim for him to wait.

"Sir," the officer spoke softly as he responded. Isaiah was still close enough to make out the conversation, "the pastor's wife said the woman threatened her with a knife."

Isaiah pulled back in surprise as the officer motioned toward him.

Tim overheard as well and his look of shock quickly turned to a scowl that he flashed at Isaiah.

The principal had heard enough; he stepped up close to the officers and cleared the anger from his face, "Officers, my mother has a mental disorder. She has a rare case of dementia and I'm afraid it is getting worse. This is no matter for the police but for a doctor, for a hospital.

I can settle her down and get to the heart of the matter. She is not dangerous, just confused."

"Sir, this is a police..." The officer was cut off by Detective Ross as the ranking officer stepped forward in front of the group of younger officers.

"Principal, how long has this been going on?"

"A few years, but it was never this bad."

"Years, you say?" Detective Ross questioned. "Regardless of her supposed condition, she is accused of threatening someone with a dangerous weapon. Would you reconsider that she might very well be dangerous given her state?"

Tim glanced at Isaiah with a stern look, then he quickly cleared the expression as he turned back to Detective Ross.

"No. She would never do something like that. No matter, though, I can resolve this situation. Let me go talk to her."

"No matter? This is a serious situation, Principal, especially for someone who works with minors."

"Yes. You're right, Detective, and let me assure you, no one wants to clear this up in a safe way more than me."

Detective Ross looked into Tim's eyes for a long moment, both men holding eye contact and not backing down.

Without Detective Ross's permission, Tim turned and walked into the house.

Detective Ross put his arm out to stop the officer behind him from walking forward to stop the principal. He allowed the principal to continue into the house.

Tim approached the door briskly and then paused before entering.

Isaiah could see the principal's shoulders rise and fall, and the man took deep breaths before he entered.

"Mom, it's me!"

He turned the door knob and walked in, softly closing the door behind him.

Five minutes seemed like hours as the officers and Isaiah were looking on toward the house.

Isaiah turned to look at the detective and found Detective Ross was already staring at him.

"What happened with my wife?" Isaiah asked.

"Appears that Mrs. Betty threatened her," he said plainly as he turned back toward the house.

The anticipation continued another moment before they were startled by a loud crash from inside the house. The officers turned to run into the house. As they approached the front door, Principal Clandes burst out of the door.

"DOCTOR! WE NEED A DOCTOR," he screamed as he pulled his mother's limp body out behind him.

Chapter 20

The Book of Zechariah

"In the past week, this church has seen a lot. I'll recap for those who may not know."

Isaiah stood behind a homemade wooden podium at the edge of center court in the high school gymnasium. His congregation sat in the pulled-out bleachers. Back in the early years, these bleachers were far from filled, but after slow and steady growth, the bleachers were close to capacity on most Sundays.

"Two of our youth were in a near-fatal car accident." He held up two fingers.

"I was arrested and held all day for questioning." He held up third finger.

"And last night, the administrator to this school tried to commit suicide. If not for the police and others already being there, she likely would have died."

He added a fourth finger to his raised hand as he stepped out from the podium and slowly looked over the crowd.

A slight smile cracked his face as he returned to the podium. "And yes, I did just say I was arrested, to all those out there wondering if you heard me right."

Isaiah brought down the four fingers on one hand and raised one finger on the other hand.

"One of those four people, in fact, one of our youth that was nearly killed in a car accident, is linked to six other young women that have *passed away*, others might use a stronger word, in recent years."

Isaiah emphasized "*passed away*" in a questioning manner as he raised both hands and turned the one finger into seven. He held it there for a moment as the crowd looked on. They were a mix of silence and stunned as they watched to see where their pastor was leading them in this sermon.

"I won't get into the details of the police questioning, but let's hold here a moment and think about this: six women dead and a seventh appears to be linked. In our town. The town where we work, live, raise our families, pray, and go to church."

He put his hands down, leaning on the podium, and caught out of the corner of his eye that Detective Ross and Principal Clandes were sitting near the doors of the gymnasium on the far side away from the crowd. They looked on and listened.

"We are living in a time of prosperity." Isaiah's tone now shifted to upbeat. "A time of prosperity, indeed." He nodded his head in unison with a portion of agreeing audience members.

"First off, the past two generations saw two of the bloodiest wars in history that spanned the globe. And thankfully, WE WON! WOO!"

The small congregation let out applause as a few men stood and cheered.

"That's right. Just over ten years ago, oh, fifteen now...fifteen years ago, we ended Nazi Germany and helped restore peace in the world." He held his fist up, squeezing it tight in celebration.

"In the years since, America has taken off like no other nation in history. Maybe closest was the Roman Empire, as it gradually expanded and prospered across the Mediterranean from Europe to the Middle East. But what happened to the Roman Empire? It's not there anymore."

Isaiah raised his shoulders and shrugged in an *I don't know* type motion.

"Well, how aligned was Rome to God?" he asked as he paused and looked over faces in the crowd.

"They helped kill Jesus, so not very aligned by my count. They rose and fell, conquering everyone in their way, even turning a blind eye to God's son, and growing too large to sustain itself in the process. Eventually, they seem to have been eaten from the inside out until the inevitable collapse.

"Does that rise and fall remind you of any other civilization?...It reminds me of the Old Testament. The Old Testament has nearly countless examples of rising and falling people...Israel."

Isaiah gripped his Bible tight behind the podium. His father's old Bible with the dark green leather and soft, warm glow that some noticed more than others.

He repeated the name as he skimmed back through his notes. "Israel."

All at once, his hand felt the burning pain that soon washed into a welcoming sensation of love and warmth. The sensation passed through his hand and into his body as it did just days ago when his father, Michael, gave it to him.

He embraced the sensation, now keeping the Bible tight in his hand as he continued to preach. "God's chosen people. They show promise, live and worship with God, then...inevitably...they make some sort of awful mistake and gradually separate from God. Whatever the method of their error, their story is the same: God anoints them, they follow him for a time, eventually they falter and must suffer the consequences, until ultimately God saves them again. It's the same old story, just with different places and faces until we get to the New Testament, but let's stay in the Old Testament today and talk more about how nations rise and fall.

"Let's suppose that every nation rises and falls at some point. Do you think America today is more like Israel before or after the Babylon exile?"

Isaiah gave pause as he looked around the congregation, studying the crowd and remembering his dreams: the children that turned into statues of ash, the sea of darkness under the giant floating Bible, the man from the fog.

"Think about it," Isaiah continued. "Before and after Babylon...In one way, we are still rising. I mean, we just won two World Wars for crying out loud. But in another way, we are so quickly drifting away from God that we may be no different from Israel, even at their worst."

Isaiah shook his head as he continued, "And every time God was there, but he allowed the fall to happen. They suffered the consequences of drifting from God, from allowing sin to take a stronger foothold in their tribe, in their nation."

His voice picked back up as he raised his volume for the next part of the sermon. "How do you like that new television? What about that second car? Oooowwwweeee! That's a nice car. How about that new job downtown that pays twice what you made before? Now you can buy that expensive cocktail and fancy wine when you take your wife to the steak house. You can talk about the latest episode of *American Bandstand*, the one you watched with your kids the night before. And while you're at dinner, those kids are having a great time at the sleepover at their friend's house, giving you and your wife the night alone so you can go on that fancy date that you earned by working those long hours."

Isaiah kept the Bible close as he returned to the podium and stood straight up, addressing the crowd as if in a one-on-one conversation.

"Prosperity. Ain't nothing wrong with making a lot of money. Nothing wrong with buying nice things with your money. That's your right, your freedom. Enjoying a show with your family."

He paused and nodded for a moment, before quickly stopping his head and then tilting it. A questioning look came across his face.

"But what are you watching on that new television? What are your children watching and filling their minds with? A show that focuses on high school kids dancing, and I mean up close and personal dancing. It also has a break halfway through for another program called *Do You Trust Your Wife?* Hmmm. Now I know that show is meant to be about how well you know each other and trivia questions, but you see where they are leading, don't you? You see the creation of lust in young minds; young minds that are already filled with hormones while the seed of marital doubt is planted in another. With each show, no matter if you are single or in a relationship, there is a line that is begging to be crossed. Temptation being dangled in front of the watchers.

"What about those long hours in your new downtown job? How many dinners have you missed in the past week so you can buy one fancy dinner for your wife a month? What are you telling your wife and kids with those actions? You're saying work is more important than them.

"What about those fancy dinners and cocktails? All good until you realize you are staying out past midnight and missing church, lying in bed the whole next day to recover.

"At least your kids are good, right? Sleeping over a friend's house? What about that older brother to your daughter's friend, do you trust him? What happens when he has a friend sleep over? I mean, if one kid gets a friend over, why not two?"

Isaiah shook his head no, back and forth.

"You can see where I'm going with this, and I don't mean to be a prude and startle you with all this as a scare tactic. Television isn't inherently evil by itself. Buying nice things isn't wrong. Kids having friends is wonderful; they need to get away from parents from time to time, and Lord knows the parents need to get away from them. I don't mean to rebuke all those things, but what I mean to do is warn you, like Zechariah warned the Israelites when they returned from exile.

"When things are going great, like when WE JUST WON A WAR! Or WE ARE FREE FROM BABYLON! YAY! It's easy to let your guard down. It's easy to drift. It's easy to lose your heart to this world one baby step at a time. And before you know it, you are being investigated in relation to six deaths, another near fatal crash, and witnessing other horrors. What is the message behind the shows you are watching? What are your kids being thrown into? What is being written on your heart? ON THEIRS?

"Don't drift. Stay true. Times of prosperity are the times to build a wall, to strengthen yourself for the eventual darkness. You cannot build a fortress after the war has already started, it's too late. Don't let the prosperity of today, the conveniences of our time lull you to sleep and into sin, eventually into destruction. It is a slippery slope. If Zechariah and Israel taught us anything, it's to stay true to God, because if we don't...the devil lurks like a hungry lion, ready to devour."

Isaiah ended the sermon and motioned to Rebecca that there were visitors near the exit. She looked to see Detective Ross and Principal Clandes before nodding to Isaiah.

Isaiah walked to the two men and greeted them.

"Thank you for coming today, gentlemen. You know, you are allowed to sit toward the center with everyone else," Isaiah said.

"Didn't want to distract you, Pastor. You were on a roll," Principal Clandes said with a smile.

"I prefer you don't speak about ongoing investigations in your sermons, Pastor," Detective Ross said with a stone face.

"Maybe these are topics we should be talking about more," Isaiah quickly retorted, holding his Bible tight in one hand at his side. "If more people knew, then it wouldn't be so easy to repeat."

"It may not be ongoing for long," the detective continued, "The situation with Mrs. Clandes, the principal's mother, has uncovered evidence linking former students at the school to the six women, the victims, and I believe you know the link to the seventh, Miss Barbara Ash, from your conversation with Mr. Gary Freed."

"Former students," Isaiah said, asking for more information.

Principal Clandes interjected, "You saw them recently, when we were in the parking lot after practice the other day. We also believe you found their clearing in the woods when you pulled Gary out on Wednesday night."

The principal paused a moment, taking a breath and steadying himself.

He continued, "My mother's condition..." he swallowed as he prepared to force the words out, choosing his words carefully, "...she was *encouraging* this group of young men to get *involved*. It seems she thought she was paying them for some sort of service to watch out for top students, especially the females. We aren't entirely sure, but with Detective Ross, we're working to uncover what happened."

Isaiah noticed Detective Ross studying Principal Clandes as he spoke.

"We will find out," the detective said confidently. "It is all coming together now in a nicely wrapped package."

Principal Clandes gave an agreeing nod, but the detective held a straight face and spoke as if the findings were uneventful. Isaiah thought to himself that the detective must love the chase but how does he feel after it all comes together? After years of no evidence and a lack of leads, the detective now had his conclusion, and it all started with an old woman that was now at the local hospital in critical condition.

Isaiah turned to Principal Clandes and saw Tim smile. It was a wincing smile, the kind you give at a funeral to say we should be happy for where the departed is going.

"Principal, how is your mother?"

"The doctors aren't sure if she is going to make it. I'm going to head back to the hospital soon. She drank a lot of bleach and the trauma from falling into the table is putting a lot of pressure on her brain. It's likely a fractured skull."

"I'm sorry to hear that. She will be in our prayers."

"Thank you. I never realized her condition was so bad, and what it could do to the community. This brings new light on the issue of dementia and mental illness."

Isaiah nodded in agreement but couldn't help to feel Tim's comment reminded him of a statement at a political rally.

"Okay, I'm back to the hospital. Pastor, I want to apologize for getting you involved with all of this. You were right about the students and I'm sorry. Also," Tim peered past Isaiah and looked at Rebecca, "please give my sincerest apologies to Rebecca. I'm sorry for all the grief and hardship my mother caused her."

"I will. And we might see you at the hospital. We are going to visit Gary and Barbara this afternoon, and if it is okay with you, we'd like to pray over your mother."

Principal Clandes looked confused. "Oh, I wouldn't expect...That's very nice of you. Of course."

The principal nodded and stepped away.

Detective Ross was silent during the exchange and watched Tim as he walked toward his car.

"How are you, Detective?" Isaiah asked, pulling the detective's attention from Tim toward Isaiah.

"Hhhmmm," the detective grunted and looked Isaiah in the eye. It was a similar look to what Detective Ross gave Isaiah during the questioning in the holding cell.

He held the look for longer than needed. Isaiah would normally have felt uncomfortable, but he gripped his Bible and stared back into the detective's eyes. He searched the detective just as Detective Ross seemed to search for an answer to an unasked question within Isaiah's pupils.

Without a word, the detective seemed to have his fill of eye contact. He turned and walked to his police cruiser.

Chapter 21

Hospital Revisited

A s they approached the hospital, Rebecca told Isaiah her disdain in seeing Mrs. Betty, even in her comatose state, after the threats the old woman made to her. But he reminded her they must be forgiving, to pray for others, and that Mrs. Betty was not in a normal mental state. Reluctantly, Rebecca agreed to pray over the woman, but only because it showed an example of forgiveness to Gary and Betty.

The nurse led them to Gary's room as Gary's father, Paul Freed, was wrapping up a conversation with Gary.

Paul pulled Isaiah aside as he stepped out of the room, "Pastor, you mind if we step outside to talk privately?"

"Of course, Paul," Isaiah responded.

As they stepped out of the room, Isaiah could hear Rebecca and Gary discussing colleges and what classes

Gary still needed to complete in his upcoming senior year.

In the hall outside Gary's room, Paul dropped his voice low.

"Are the rumors true?" he asked Isaiah.

"What rumors?"

"That Mrs. Betty is a crazy old lady who was paying guys to kill girls," Paul said softly and directly, with a forceful tone in his voice.

"I don't know if I'd phrase it that way. Did you know Ms. Betty has a mental condition? Who knows what she thought she was doing or if those men took advantage of her."

"Oh yeah, give me a break, Pastor," Paul responded quickly. "Did she ever seem out of it to you? I saw her nearly every week and she was the same stuck-up old broad, hellbent on making her son look good and keeping those kids in line."

Paul shook his head before continuing, "Did you know she used to love Gary, LOVE HIM. But after this past football season, she gave him the cold shoulder. She would compliment him and welcome him when he went in to see the principal, which was Tim's idea, by the way, to mentor the boy when he got the starting QB job. But after the poor season, nothing but disdain. She acted like he was a plague on the school. Now I ain't saying it's their fault, Lord knows I'm not the perfect father, but Gary's attitude and depression started when that lady undercut him every time she saw him. And I hate to be the one to say, but someone has to, that mean old lady got what was coming to her."

"Paul, come on now. She tried committing suicide and may have succeeded."

"Yeah, yeah," Paul said bitterly. "All I know is I'm not going to forget who she was. And just because she might die doesn't mean I have to rewrite her history. Before her and her son arrived, the school may not have had the highest test scores and state champion athletics, but at least we had peace. That school has been a bed of evil for years."

"We are all shaken up a bit. It's been a tough week."

"OH CUT THE CRAP, PASTOR," Paul retorted violently. Two nearby nurses looked over, but Isaiah nodded and put his hands up, signaling everything was okay.

He turned back to Paul, who was only inches away from his face, and dropped his voice back to a softer volume.

"Is this what you called me out here for? To bad-mouth an old woman with dementia? I spoke with the police. They are going after the people that Mrs. Betty led them to. They are going to get the men who murdered others on her behalf."

"Yes," Paul said plainly, "but it's not just that. You need to open your eyes. Get educated. That woman may be dead soon, and I heard those four men are already in police custody, but even so, there is something wrong here."

Paul looked away, slightly shaking his head in disbelief.

He continued, "I love this city, but we're not staying. Once Gary is well enough, we're moving up north, closer to family. We're getting away from whatever is going on here. My son won't finish high school in this...this SEA OF DARKNESS."

Sea of Darkness.

Isaiah's mind went to his dream.

The waves of black water, splashing against the giant Bible as people stood on it.

It was Isaiah's people. Or at least the man from the fog had said as much, the man who called Isaiah his father.

Sea of Darkness...Isaiah's mind left the conversation with Paul and was locked on the black waves.

Paul continued and Isaiah snapped back to the present moment. "That's what I wanted to tell you. We're leaving. And that you need to keep your eyes open, or you're going to drown here."

Paul turned and opened the door to Gary's hospital room. "Hey son, be back in a couple hours with your mom and dinner. Have a good one, Mrs. Light."

He turned and walked down the hall as Isaiah still saw the black waves rise and fall in his mind. He also remembered his other dream, where the children burned into charcoal statues that grew and grew, overtaking him.

The Bible had shined the light that blasted away the ash.

The Bible.

It was the source of light in one dream that broke the darkness and a raft in the sea of darkness in the other.

Both dreams, the same Bible, the same light beat out similar darkness.

A nurse passed by Isaiah and spoke up. "Sir, please do not linger in the halls. Please find your room or return to the waiting area."

Isaiah nodded and stepped halfway into Gary's room before being reminded of the other reason Rebecca and he came to the hospital, to see Mrs. Betty.

"Excuse me, nurse? Nurse," Isaiah called out as he trotted a few quick steps behind the passing nurse.

"Yes?"

"Could you tell where Mrs. Betty Clandes' room is?"

"Oh, I'm sorry, you didn't hear?"

Isaiah shook his head no and quivered his eyebrows.

"I'm sorry to have to tell you this, sir, but she passed on."

Isaiah slowly nodded. "Thank you, nurse."

He slowly turned to exit the hallway when a doorway ahead of him opened.

It was a hospital bed being pushed by an orderly. Two men walked next to it as they talked: a doctor and Principal Clandes.

The sheets on the bed were pulled up over the face and head of the person lying on it.

Mrs. Betty.

They passed by Isaiah and Principal Tim looked up with a somber expression.

He noticed Isaiah and his expression tightened into a solemn, blank face. He locked eyes with Isaiah as he paused the conversation with the doctor.

The doctor raised his arm in response to stop the orderly.

Tim walked around his mother's body and stepped to Isaiah.

"Pastor, I'm...I'm afraid my mother has passed on."

"I'm sorry, Tim."

"I'd like services to be later this week and wanted to know if you and your wife would be there to read a prayer and preside over her burial?"

"Absolutely."

"Thank you, Pastor. I need a few days but how about lunch on Wednesday to discuss and finalize the details? Same place as yesterday where Detective Ross found us, BBQ?"

"Of course."

Principal Tim sniffed and wiped the corner of his eye with a knuckle wrapped in tissue. He corrected his posture and returned to the hospital bed. They moved down the hall, following signs to the hospital morgue.

Rebecca came out of Gary's room and stepped up behind Isaiah, holding his arm in hers.

"Mrs. Betty?"

Isaiah shook his head yes. "Tim asked if we could be at the service later this week. I don't think he knows any other pastors."

As the bed was pushed out of sight, Rebecca noticed an open doorway down the hall.

It was Barbara's room.

She was in a wheelchair, stuck in between a half-closed door.

"Barbara," Rebecca said as she jogged to help the girl.

Isaiah followed, and as they approached, they saw she was not stuck, but instead she was trying to hide. She seemed paralyzed and afraid to move.

Tears poured down her face in her silent fear as the bottom of her headgear held a swaying tear and the collar of her hospital gown was damp from the crying.

Her eyes were fixed down the hallway, and outside her streaming tears, she was as motionless as a statue.

She looked in the direction of Mrs. Betty's bed as it rolled to the morgue.

Chapter 22

The Seventh Day

One week after Michael Light gave his son the family Bible, it saved Isaiah's life.

The dreams rolled through Isaiah's mind every night until he met Principal Clandes for a late lunch on Wednesday afternoon. He now carried the Bible with him everywhere he went, thinking it would give him inspiration for the meaning of the dreams, and he had it under his arm as he arrived at Pete's BBQ for lunch.

Tim was already there, sitting at a picnic table, and was the only one present at the BBQ stand.

Isaiah approached Tim, looking at the empty area with confusion. "Is it closed today?"

"Sort of. They closed early for a special catering event, but I called ahead and our meals are being kept warm. Please sit. I'll grab them."

As Tim stood up, Isaiah sat and spoke before Tim walked away. "I hope you don't mind, but I invited someone else. Jimmy Job; you know him, right?"

Tim looked disturbed for a moment. "I thought it was going to be just us? We are talking about my mother's funeral."

"I can ask him to leave, it's no problem."

"No, no," Tim said as Jimmy's car pulled up. "It's okay; we'll deal with him then as well."

"Deal with?"

"Oh, I just meant that I only ordered two meals in advance, but let me grab another plate and we'll divide it up. Should be enough, two pounds of brisket. I hope you like it moist."

Isaiah smiled as Jimmy approached.

In truth, Isaiah had not invited Jimmy; Rebecca did.

When Isaiah told her about his conversation with Paul, she felt for Paul's concern and wanted to make sure Isaiah used the buddy system wherever he went. That meant Jimmy joining him for lunch.

Isaiah protested and felt like she was overreacting, but Rebecca held her ground.

In the end, she asked Isaiah what would be the difference between having a good friend right there with him. Plus, she argued that with Tim's growing business and political leadership, it'd be good for him and Jimmy to connect. Isaiah couldn't argue and reluctantly agreed.

Isaiah smiled at Jimmy as he approached and they both took a seat at the picnic table.

Tim came around from the back of the smoker hut holding a large ceramic platter filled with beef brisket and cornbread in one hand, while he balanced paper plates, plastic forks, and a bottle of BBQ sauce in his other hand.

"Wow," Isaiah said as Tim put the platter on the wooden table.

Tim turned to Jimmy. "Mr. Job, right? Been a long time, a few years at least."

"Yes, sir, and please call me Jimmy. Thank you for lunch," Jimmy said as he motioned to the platter.

"Of course, of course. You have a boy at my school, is that right? And you are the boxer, a fighter if I'm not mistaken?"

"Not yet, but young James Jr. will be there soon. And fighting was a lifetime ago. I prefer to think of myself as a Christian and family man at Isaiah's church," he motioned to Isaiah, "long, long before fighting comes into my identity."

"Fair enough. I have to say, though, I have such respect for those who get in the ring. The training and discipline required, literally fighting other competitors to accomplish greatness, to face off one-to-one with your opponent. Amazing."

They grew quiet as the food was distributed and they began eating.

The normally quiet Jimmy was the first to speak as he motioned to Tim. "I'm sorry about your mother, sir. My family gives its condolences and you are in our prayers."

"Thank you," Tim said and paused. "This past week has been a difficult one. I never thought it'd happen like this."

Isaiah and Jimmy nodded as the three of them continued eating.

"This has been my favorite BBQ for years," Tim said as the platter began to disappear, "Did you know that he was going to expand?"

"Really?" Isaiah asked.

Tim continued, "That's right. I even connected him with businessmen I work with through the Chamber of Commerce. They were interested in investing to make it happen, but Pete backed out."

"No way," Isaiah responded in question.

Tim nodded. "Said he liked how things were, didn't want to let *'his love of the food'* get interrupted with the business. Wanted to keep it simple."

"I suppose that is understandable," Isaiah said, shrugging.

"Yeah, I suppose...but foolish."

Isaiah was mildly surprised by the principal's bluntness. "You think so?"

"Yup, foolish. This area is growing rapidly. The entire state is growing in population faster than most spots in the nation. Now is the time to get your footing to capitalize on it. You see what they're doing down in Orlando? All that land for family parks? A *'Theme Park.'* All that money, from lots of powerful people, is betting that Florida is going to be taking off. Lawmakers are even clearing the way for investments, adding taxes to tourism instead of on the business side. That's smart. But Pete doesn't realize his own potential. It's sad."

"You know a lot about business. More than I would expect from a principal."

"I stay in touch," Tim said confidently. "How is your wife, by the way? I am looking forward to having her at my mother's funeral."

"She's good," Isaiah said curiously. "But let's talk about the funeral service. I don't know the day, time, or place yet. And is there a certain style of message or sermon, or specific memories from her life you want me to highlight?"

Tim paused for a moment, looking at Isaiah with a blank expression. He seemed to be thinking of a memory. He shifted his gaze to Jimmy, then back to Isaiah, and nodded his head a few short beats, as if coming to a conclusion.

"She served her purpose well. That's what I'll remember her for most. And it is really tragic she won't be able to see what goes atop the foundation she built."

Isaiah looked at Tim and remained silent. He always saw Principal Clandes as political and very careful with his words. Now Tim spoke more authentically, more easily and confidently than Isaiah had experienced with him.

"And no rush on the service details," Tim stated. "It will likely be delayed."

Jimmy caught Isaiah's eye. Jimmy was slowly shaking his head no and Isaiah could see him clenching his fist.

In a flash, a revelation dawned on Isaiah: Mrs. Betty, Barbara, Gary, the men in the parking lot, the connection between the seven women.

Rebecca's pet peeve of when Mrs. Betty used *"we"* instead of *"I."* Mrs. Betty was talking on someone else's behalf. She was a messenger when she visited Rebecca.

Barbara was petrified when the hospital bed rolled past her; she wasn't scared of Mrs. Betty.

The men in the woods and in the parking lot watching practice. It wasn't Ms. Betty talking with them.

The drive for school ratings and top-tier athletics came from the top, led by recruiting the best and brightest, frequently young women from surrounding areas.

Gary's depression coincided with being mentored.

No one saw Mrs. Betty commit suicide, except for one person who was in the house with her.

One person was at the center of it all...

Isaiah's face tightened as he looked at Principal Clandes in a new light.

Principal Clandes saw Isaiah's expression change, he noticed Jimmy's fist clench, and he seemed to welcome it.

Tim smiled as he slowly picked up the empty ceramic platter.

In a flash, he swung it at Jimmy.

Jimmy instinctively raised an arm in defense, but it was too late to fully block the blow.

The thick ceramic shattered over his head and shoulder. The sharp edges from the broken platter ripped into the side of Jimmy's head, above his ear, and below his shoulder near his triceps. Skin and muscles flapped off his arm as Jimmy went down, unconscious off the side of the picnic table.

As Isaiah stood, he brought with him the Bible that was in his lap.

Principal Tim turned his body, and in a fast, fluid motion, he threw what remained of the sharp platter at Isaiah's face.

Isaiah raised his arms in time, the bulk of the platter's force was deflected by the Bible, protecting his face but slicing his forearm. The force pushed him off balance as the back of his knees gave way to the wooden seat behind them.

He fell backward, with a bleeding forearm on one arm and still holding the Bible tight in the other, he turned to see Jimmy and a small pool of blood beginning to form around him in the hard gravel. Both men were lying on the ground, losing blood fast, while Timothy Clandes stood up calmly from his seat.

Isaiah turned his head away from Jimmy and toward the principal in time to see a black boot swing at his head.

The boot struck the top of his head and Isaiah saw a flash of light as he was dazed by the kick, but still conscious.

Tim bent down and grabbed his collar. He began dragging Isaiah to the nearby road. The same deceiving turn that Gary and Barbara had crashed on, where visibility was limited from the road and the speed limit remained high through the bend.

"You just couldn't stop, could you? I left you alone, but you had to keep poking around, messing with my school, my town, my future," Principal Tim said bitterly as he dragged Isaiah through the grass.

"You kept asking questions and wouldn't shut up, and then calling out my mother...well, maybe I should thank you for that. That foolish detective was getting too close and Mother had to go sooner or later. So...yes, thank you for that." He turned, letting Isaiah's collar loose as he kicked Isaiah's side swiftly with his boot.

Isaiah felt a crack and winced with the pain. His body could hardly move, but his mind was finally coming to after the blow to his head.

"It will be fun going after Rebecca," Tim said coldly, mocking Isaiah. "Even before all this, I had my eye on her. I wanted a church woman by my side for the upcoming election, but Joan, no, no, she didn't work at all. She was like the rest."

Tim continued to pull Isaiah toward the upcoming road. The sound of cars and trucks shooting past began to deafen Tim's comments out of Isaiah's hearing.

He turned and looked up as Tim dragged him and continued his rant.

"Yes, Rebecca will do well. You will be dead and the police will find evidence that you had a relationship with Joan; that'll start to turn her in my direction. You wouldn't believe how easily a comment made in the right way can lead to 'evidence.' And my mother will be dead of a horrible mental illness that led to her suicide. We will both need to find solace, and I'll be there for her."

"No," Isaiah spouted out with a cough.

Tim Clandes stopped dragging Isaiah, let loose his collar, and slowly turned to look down on the pastor.

"No? NO," Tim screamed as anger overtook his face before it quickly subsided. His voice returned to the matter-of-fact nature he previously spoke in. "You act like you have a say in the matter. This is in motion, all of it. You're gone. Your friend Jimmy will be next. Too bad he can't take a hit anymore. I thought he would be harder to knock down. Maybe I'll let them find his body so his kids can see. That'd be a good lesson for them. Nosy wife and little brats."

"No," Isaiah forced out again.

Tim looked down. An annoyed look came across his face.

"No, huh? And what are you going to do about it?"

The anger returned to Tim's face as he kicked Isaiah in the same cracked rib.

Searing pain shot through Isaiah's body as he struggled to catch his breath.

The kick rolled him to his belly. Sweat and blood rolled down his face and dripped off his nose into the hot sand that now caked his hands. The last kick had forced all his air out as he gasped to bring it back. Pushing up, he slowly moved off the ground.

"Go ahead, GET UP," Tim screamed. His patience was at its end and the anger stayed. His true colors were showing above the facade he portrayed on a daily basis to the world.

Another kick came hard and fast to Isaiah's midsection, *TTTHHUUUDDD*, and the pain increased yet again, now pulsing through his body. More ribs cracked.

Raising one hand to protect his head, he saw Jimmy, his closest friend, lying motionless, blood pooling around his arm and head where two deep gashes were opened.

Jimmy needed medical attention, so did Isaiah.

Tim switched back and forth from kicking Isaiah to pushing him with the bottom of his large black boot, using it to shove Isaiah. He pushed at his head and shoulders, moving him closer to the busy road ahead of them. They were blocked to the speeding drivers by the upcoming curve and overgrown shrubs.

"I knew this day would come," he said bitterly to the pastor, with an air of superiority in his voice.

TTTHHUUDD, another kick, this time to Isaiah's shoulder.

TTTHHUUDD, yet another, now aimed at his head.

Isaiah's arm absorbed part of the blow, but the impact to his skull left him once again dazed as if a grenade went off nearby and stunned his senses.

"You just had to keep asking questions about Joan, then Gary, and then Barbara. You just couldn't accept the answers."

The voice was muffled in Isaiah's ringing ear.

Isaiah felt so naive. All this time, the common thread of all the hurt people. Rebecca's instinct. Paul's comment on the Sea of Darkness.

It was right in front of him, but he didn't see it.

He underestimated the evil in the world, never thinking it would come for him or his wife or their church.

This was evil in human form, not sinful human nature of greed or jealousy or lust; this was beyond that.

It was preying on the young adults of the community, and he, then Jimmy, then Rebecca were next. Who knew how many bodies it racked up as it fulfilled its pleasures, or how many would be yet to come.

TTTHHUUDD, another shot to Isaiah's midsection.

Isaiah winced at the pain, but his senses were returning. His mind began to come back.

He thought he must stand up. Somehow. He must help Jimmy. He could not let this evil go on. He must return to Rebecca.

TTTHHUUDD

"You want to get up? Go ahead, GET UP!"

Another kick came.

Toying with him.

Pushing him closer toward the road.

Inviting him to rise.

As he guarded his head against the blows, he realized his Bible was underneath him. He had it when the surprise attack first hit Jimmy, and it was under his arm when Tim threw the broken platter at him.

He unconsciously held on to it, protected it, and gripped it tight even while nearly unconscious. Now he still had it through the struggle.

His dreams flashed in his mind as he came to from the previous blow to his head.

The Bible blasted away the suffocating statues of ash, of death.

The Bible was the life raft that Isaiah's people stood on. The Bible.

It was with him the whole time, and now its soft glow stood out in the dirt and the blood.

The glow coming from the spine caught Isaiah's attention. If he didn't make it out of this, he would never be able to talk to his father about it. Never be able to learn about what his father had given him.

His attacker wouldn't let him live.

Another push from his attacker's leg, inching Isaiah closer to the busy highway road ahead.

In the scramble of the attack, he instinctively protected the book, and the book began to protect him. He focused all his attention on the glowing light.

The blows came harder and faster, he was now right above the shoulder of the road, nearly out of the shrubs that blocked them from passing drivers, but Isaiah didn't feel the same pain as he once did.

Tim screamed, "Still can't GET UP," as he dropped an elbow on Isaiah's back, snapping another bone.

But Isaiah didn't wince.

Tim began pulling Isaiah off the ground, preparing to throw him into the road. The busy road with the deceiving turn, leading to many crashes and arguments in city debates over the safety of the area. The drivers wouldn't be able to respond in time to get out of the way.

As the attacker pulled Isaiah up, his Bible and the warm glow gave him strength.

His resolve sharpened.

He had been protecting the book. Protecting the mil-lennia-old secret hidden in its bindings that he remained unaware of.

In the chaos of the moment, the book seemed to speak to him. To teach him what he never grasped on his own.

He had been protecting the book, but he was never meant to protect the book.

The book was meant to protect him.

It was his weapon against the evils of this world.

The last seven days were his education, his trial by fire, his preparation for the coming fight.

Isaiah shrugged and broke loose from Tim's grip as the principal grabbed a fistful of Isaiah's shirt. Tim pulled Isaiah back with one hand and struck Isaiah's mid-section with the other, hitting the already damaged rib cage.

But Isaiah hardly felt the pain.

He used the motion to roll away from Tim and in the process swung his elbow, catching Tim in the side of his jaw.

The elbow struck hard and Tim released Isaiah's shirt as he held his chin and stumbled backward. A mix of surprise and pain flooded the principal's face.

Isaiah escaped Tim's grasp, but now he stood in be-tween the road and Tim. With his back to the road, one push and he'd face a vehicle head-on.

Tim's face tightened and reddened, furious with being hit back. He motioned to strike Isaiah, but Isaiah held up the Bible. The soft glow distracted Tim and paused him before he struck again.

Isaiah used the opportunity. He jabbed at Tim, catching his right eye with a quick hard strike that Jimmy would have been proud of.

Again, Tim moved to strike but was too slow in the light of the glow. Isaiah punched again, this time catching Tim's nose as he stumbled backward.

Blood began streaming down Tim's nose, over his lips and down his chin.

The fury and anger in Tim's eyes now turned to enjoyment as he smiled wide with blood-covered teeth. He'd praised boxing only a moment before, and now he was enjoying the battle, the strikes, the pain.

Tim's eyes opened wide and he charged. He couldn't throw an unconscious Isaiah into oncoming traffic like he had planned, but he would still make sure the pastor ended up there.

Tim stepped forward and charged with a scream. The sound was full of anger, but Isaiah saw a slight smile, an enjoyment of the violence, on Tim's face.

He was unleashing his true self, no longer in his make-believe public persona.

The rage-filled scream carried across the grassy area, into the parking lot.

Behind Tim's charge, back in the picnic area, two figures caught Isaiah's eye.

Jimmy was crawling past the tables and into the dirt. Even in his weakened state, he was trying to help Isaiah.

Behind Jimmy, Detective Ross's car pulled into the parking lot. Far from the situation, Isaiah saw the man swing out of his car and begin to sprint.

Tim charged, ready to shove Isaiah into oncoming traffic before turning on Jimmy and any others in his way.

Isaiah bent down quickly, ducking his head while raising the Bible to cover his head like a Spartan warrior raising his shield to ward off the onslaught of a charging foe.

Tim's momentum carried him above Isaiah. The attacker tried to adjust, raising a knee in an attempt to blow through the Bible and split Isaiah's skull.

But the knee never touched the Bible.

The soft glow of the Bible was more than a light coming out of the binding.

It was protection.

Tim's knee abruptly stopped, as if it was hitting an invisible forcefield, and was pushed up as the momentum carried it. His leg seemed to run from the force within the book, as if every molecule within Tim's skin, muscle, and bone tried to escape. The knee hyperextended, as the joint bent the wrong way. His leg remained attached, but the force of the book turned it to more of a molded clay as the knee deformed, the hip shifted, and the foot contorted backward.

Tim's momentum combined with the repellent force of the Bible carried him over Isaiah like a bike launching off a ramp.

Isaiah lifted his head in time to see his attacker directly above him. In that split second, Isaiah saw a fear in Tim's eyes that he would never forget. The face of confusion and realization, realizing the power of the book and the impact it had on his body. Tim's momentum carried him further into the glow of the book as he passed over Isaiah, his leg deflecting off and deforming, then his hip, and now his midsection and arm coming into the glow and deforming like clay just like his leg.

His entire body caught between his momentum, gravity, and the glow, the force of the book, as each cell was seemingly running away from the force, abandoning their physical presence to resist the light at all costs.

Isaiah's mind went to the ash statues of his dream: The light blasted away the darkness.

The black waves in the Sea of Darkness: The light forced them back.

Tim was now the darkness, and he had no fight against the light.

The principal landed on the road behind Isaiah and struck the hot pavement with a dull thud.

Isaiah stood and looked into Timothy Clandes' eyes.

A trembling fear seemed to fill the mangled body as he tried standing up, not realizing the extent of damage to its major joints and muscles.

Tim stumbled, unable to stand in his new deformed body.

He picked his head up and flashed a look of confusion at Isaiah, of heartbreak. He opened his mouth but before he could push breath from his lungs, a cement truck plowed through him.

The collision splattered blood and body across the road.

The large truck didn't stop.

It kept driving through the dangerous bend and over the river, out of sight.

Tim's body was a mere pothole to the truck as it sped out of sight.

Isaiah stood, still holding his Bible firmly in one hand and looking at the spot of stained road where Timothy Clandes once lay.

Isaiah thanked the Lord.

He turned to see Jimmy, who was still crawling toward Isaiah to help. A trail of blood followed Jimmy from the parking lot through the grass and dirt. Jimmy had crawled on his knees and one arm, like a determined three-legged dog that wouldn't be stopped, but at the sight of Principal Tim's deformed body, he stopped and stared in awe at what he just witnessed.

Detective Ross also stood motionless, in wonder, questioning if his eyes really saw what he thought he did.

Isaiah approached Jimmy and helped him up.

As Jimmy stood up, his hand grabbed Isaiah's arm that held the Bible. Jimmy felt a painful sensation he never felt before, followed by a warming, loving sensation.

It was the same sensation that Isaiah felt when he first took the Bible from his father. The pain, like mini daggers, as parts of himself seemed to run away from the book, but also a welcoming warmth that soon followed.

But Jimmy wasn't touching the Bible; he felt the sensation through Isaiah's arms as his friend helped him up.

They stepped toward Detective Ross, Isaiah helping Jimmy secure his damaged arm.

Behind Detective Ross, other squad cars piled into the parking lot, followed by an ambulance.

Detective Ross was speechless.

Isaiah smiled a polite and welcoming smile to the detective.

Chapter 23

Next

Isaiah spent the next two days in bed, only getting up to go to the kitchen or restroom. On Friday afternoon, the phone woke Isaiah. He rolled over, still feeling pain in his ribs, and put a pillow over his head as Rebecca had a short conversation.

After the call, Rebecca came into the room and sat at the bedside. Isaiah, unable to return to sleep, painfully rolled to his back and smiled at his wife.

Rebecca smiled back.

Isaiah began, "You know, I never called Detective Ross to thank him for showing up."

"You should call Dixie and thank her," Rebecca responded.

"Dixie?"

"Yeah, after you and Jimmy had gone to lunch, I called Dixie for a ride to my doctor's appointment. Once we got to talking about Mrs. Betty, she called the police and said they needed to be there. She knows Detective Ross and asked for him personally."

"Maybe we can have them over for dinner soon." Isaiah smiled thankfully. "Have you heard any updates on Jimmy?"

"Ended up being forty-five stitches. Twenty on the side of his head, twenty-five down his arm," she said as used her index finger to run a line across Isaiah's head and arm to show where.

"He seems to be up and moving again," she continued.

"That's not surprising. He never stays down."

"Dixie said she had to withhold dinner just to get him to cancel this weekend's slate of open houses. He needs to rest, and so do you."

Rebecca brought up the covers and tucked Isaiah back in bed as she kissed his forehead.

"Yes, ma'am," Isaiah said as he squirmed in bed, trying to find a comfortable way to lie. His three broken ribs made it impossible to be comfortable. "Was that Dixie who called just now?"

"Nope," she said, smiling, nearly laughing as she appeared to hold back a joke.

"Okay...Who was it?"

Rebecca took a deep breath and let it out with a happy *Aaaahhhh* sound in a long exhale as she enjoyed playfully making her husband wait.

"Well," she continued, "that's what I came to talk to you about. It was the doctor."

"The doctor? About Gary or Barbara?"

"Nope," she said smugly. "Different doctor."

"And..." Isaiah rolled his hand in circles, gesturing to her to explain.

"I'm pregnant."

Isaiah didn't move except for blinking repeatedly.

"What?" he mouthed without saying the words as a broad smile came across his face.

"I'm pregnant. You are going to be a dad."

"And you're going to BE A MOTHER!" Isaiah lifted out of bed as he screamed and hugged his wife before painfully retreating back from the movement on his broken ribs.

They kissed and stared silently at each other for a long moment.

Watery eyes left a tear of joy running down Rebecca's face.

They embraced in a long hug, as much as Isaiah could bear, until he broke the silence.

"So Isaiah Jr., that has a nice ring to it, eh?"

"Oh, please. You can convince me of a Bible name, but we're not doing a junior."

"Well, if it's a boy, let's start with the main four: Matthew, Mark, Luke, and John are your choices."

"Hmmm, well, I was thinking..." She moved her hand from holding Isaiah's arm to the Bible on the nightstand next to the bed. She rubbed the dark green leather and noticed the slight glow from the inner binding. "Ever since you spoke on Zechariah, that name has stuck with me...And I had this strange dream we were standing on your Bible, and well, I feel like we already met him."

Isaiah blinked in amazement.

She smiled at the Bible and then turned to see his reaction.

Isaiah nodded as he grinned. "I love it. Baby Zech."

"And if it's a girl, then it'll be Elizabeth to match my mother," Rebecca quickly shot out.

"Of course, of course," Isaiah agreed.

"Zechariah," she smiled, "I like that."

Chapter 24

Epilogue

Eight months later, after three surgeries and many painful hours of therapy, Gary held a cane tight as he walked out of the hospital. His parents waited for him next to their car while Barbara and James Jr. stood close by and cheered him on as he broke the threshold of the exit door.

Barbara was released from the hospital weeks after the incident between Isaiah and Principal Clandes. Her headgear came off after three months and she eventually was able to talk again. Her broken jaw left her with a speech impediment, but it was gradually being improved through speech lessons and practice with her mother. She would go on to sing in the church choir and in her later years, and none of the younger women believed she once had an impediment.

Soon after Barbara's release, she joined James Jr. in regular visits to the hospital. The two visited Gary at least two to three times every week, usually bringing with them the lesson from that week's youth group, board games, school work, or dropping off and picking up books on Gary's behalf from the local library.

Before long, Barbara and Gary were officially boyfriend and girlfriend again and Gary convinced his father to wait out his senior year before moving the family up north. Ultimately, Gary's parents never ended up moving and they returned to being active members at the Lights' church, however, Gary and Barbara did move.

The young couple was married six months after high school graduation. Gary would spend ten years in the Army, including two deployments to Vietnam that moved Gary and Barbara around the country, eventually settling in Texas, where Gary began a successful trucking company.

Gary and Barbara had two children, a daughter named Ruth and a son named Robert. Ruth met her future husband at a church conference back in her parents' hometown of Jacksonville, and after many long car rides and letters back and forth, he proposed to her and she moved back to the North Florida area.

She and her husband, Micah Grey, had one child.

Jeremiah Grey.

Continue the story generations later with the full Light of the Ark series, starting with Book 1: Light of the Ark.

Next Up - Free Preview!

Finally, before you go, I'd like to thank you for reading by giving you the first chapter of **Christian's Look Back at Life,** a psychological thriller with a Christian twist:

> The horrible accident left Christian Flagler with an amazing gift. He can relive any moment from his past just by thinking about it. The smell of his wife's perfume the day they married. The smack of the baseball as he plays catch with his son.

> Stuck in the past, he grows distant from those he loves. Every day, he walks the sleepy town reminded of what he lost. The gift has become a curse.

> Until one day, he finds a special center that treats people with his condition. His new sponsor, Michael, helps Christian get out of his rut as they look back on his life through

his unique gift. But easier said than done, as dark forces do not want Christian to change.

To win the fight ahead, Christian must leave his past behind.

Please continue on to see the full first chapter. I hope you enjoy it.

JAMES BONK

CHRISTIAN'S
LOOK BACK AT
LIFE

A CHRISTIAN FICTION NOVELLA
ON LIFE AND DEATH

Hello, Christian

"Hello, Christian. Welcome."

"Please, call me Chris."

"Chris. It's nice to meet you. I know you didn't get a choice in picking your sponsor, and to be honest, we don't get to choose as well, but I've looked over your material and I expect us to do well together."

"I...I don't mean to be rude," Chris said as he fidgeted with his hands, "but I don't really need these extra sessions. Is there an assigned reading or something like that I can do? I don't want to waste your time, and I'm sure you can help plenty of others, the people who really need it."

"That's nice of you to think of others. But to answer your question, no, there is no further reading than what you have already seen. And I disagree with you; this is exactly what you need. It's why you're here, and it's why I'm here."

Chris looked away from Michael as his arms loosely crossed and his shoulders slouched forward.

"Please, have a seat." Michael motioned to the orange plastic chair that sat in the middle of the giant room with wooden floors. It was Chris's old high school gymnasium, where he could still remember first-period Personal Fitness class from nearly thirty years ago. It was also the same high school where Chris's son, Jake, was currently a senior.

Chris shuffled his feet, reluctantly kicking them forward with every step. He was forty-six years old but always felt like a small boy in these sessions, like they forced him to sit in the dentist's chair and endure painful drilling.

Michael was the second "sponsor" that Chris had met in the past five years at the modest mental health organization. They focused on helping those with rare mental disorders, and Chris had never heard of anyone in his condition prior to coming here.

Five years ago, Chris was in a horrible traffic accident involving multiple cars. A strange condition developed immediately afterwards in which he could remember every moment in his life before the accident. From the most mundane to the most extreme, all he had to do was close his eyes and think about it, and he'd instantly be there, reliving it for as long as he wished until deciding to return to the exact moment he closed his eyes. It was hardly longer than a blink in his current situation, but he could be gone for hours, days, months on end if so compelled.

At first, it felt like a superpower. He could walk by the grocery store and remember walking through it with his wife and son. He remembered the exact items, the exact price, and the exact time of day that Jake would help him put into the cart. But it was more than a photographic memory; he could remember his feelings, his thoughts, every single detail of the situation: the smell of the rotisserie chickens as he walked into the grocery store, the fresh and colorful berries in the produce section, the smooth surface of the wine bottle as he picked it up and balanced the weight, and all the times his wife squeezed his arm tight to stay close.

As he walked past structures in the small, overcast town, he relived joyful moments over and over. The Super Bowl party back in his twenties with his soon-to-be wife as they watched his favorite team close out the big win. They were dating exactly a month at the time and he remembered forgetting the game when she kissed him in celebration. It was his first memory of love for his wife. She cared nothing for football, yet was as emotionally invested in the game as he was, sitting on the edge of their seats during the plays and laughing off the tension during the highly anticipated commercials.

Other moments, such as golfing with his best friends. The joyful explosion when he sank the twenty-foot chip shot to save par for their group. The agony of landing three straight shots in the water as his friends ribbed his wild drives.

However, as time went on, he spent more time in his head, remembering related moments of the past and being less in the moment. Gradually, he grew distant from his family. Whatever happened, he had a corresponding memory to slip off into, returning in body but unable to communicate the emotions from the past.

His son was twelve at the time of the accident, and in the prior five years, they played catch or tag or whatever game of the season in their backyard countless times. However, in the five years since, zero. Chris couldn't even say "countless" anymore when he thought of playing with his boy. Given his mysterious condition, he went back and lived each moment. He knew that in the five years before his accident, he and Jake played in their backyard exactly nine hundred and thirteen times. He had the tallies on notepaper to prove it, averaging once every two days.

Chris would relive the first time his son learned to throw a spiral, the first time he gave the baseball enough power for Chris's palm to tingle in pain, or the first time he put a spin on the soccer ball and watched it bend in the air. That was one of Chris's proudest moments, watching his son figure out not only the strength but the finesse required to put the proper spin on the ball. But after years of missing playtime, Jake was more wrapped up in his team sports, his friends, his own life. Father-son time was gone.

The gap between Chris and his only child was not the only growing divide in the family. Chris and his wife, Evelyn, stopped communicating as well. Evelyn tried, Chris knew she was doing her best as night after night she would talk to herself as she willed Chris to care, to respond, to just be there. She would cry about how she missed him, for him to say something, say anything. But every time, Chris was speechless. He tried...he really did. But every fight led him into a memory. He'd return and know it'd all be fine. It would be okay. Evelyn would understand, she'd come around. She always did.

When he moved out of the house, there was not a huge fight. No thrown dishes and curses. He didn't sit down with his son to tell him he still loved him, that he missed him and his mother. He never told Jake that it wasn't his fault, that sometimes things just don't work out. There was none of that. One day, Chris packed what he could carry and walked out of the house.

He didn't go far, renting an apartment just over a mile away, but the communication remained closed. Every time he looked at the phone, he thought of calling. But every time he thought of it, he didn't want to bother them; he would see them soon.

It would be okay...until it wasn't.

After he moved out, Chris walked more than ever. Sunrise and sunset were his favorite times of the day. He liked to think it was the colorful skies and chilly temperatures that kept him out for hours at a time on most days, but deep down, he knew it was the lonesome apartment that he wanted to avoid.

He'd walk by the local coffee shops and pizzerias, by the ever-rotating corner stores that seemed to shift from fashion boutique to frozen yogurt to whatever new attempt at commerce that the season brought with it.

His most joyful, yet most painful, walk of each day was when he turned down the main road of his old neighborhood.

Most days, he wouldn't go into the subdivision, but every week or two, he mustered up the courage to stroll past the gates and walk down his old street. He was never sure if he wanted to see Evelyn or Jake. What would he say if they saw him? Nothing, he thought to himself. Nothing - PERIOD. He spent years not saying anything, so why should this time be any different?

Yet, his former home still drew him in as he remembered more of good times than the bad. The tickle fights with a five-year-old Jake. Picking up Evelyn and spinning her around when she hung up the call that announced her big promotion.

As much as he tried to stay in the wonderful moments, he could not avoid drifting into regrets. The time he broke the lock on Jake's door after the boy slammed the door in his face. He spanked the boy as hard as he could that night. The boy wasn't rebelling; he was just upset. Chris was upset himself, but Chris lost it and slapped his bottom so hard, his hand hurt.

The sad memories of Evelyn: fights over money, forgetting their fifth anniversary, all those weekends where he just *had* to go into work. He never cleared the air after a fight with Evelyn; they eventually came to an unspoken understanding and went to sleep, restarting the next day fresh.

The memory of Evelyn was the reason he first entered the facility and met his introductory sponsor. He tried to avoid that memory—it ate at him—but seeing his friends at a local restaurant/bar, *The Evening Lounge*, helped him deal with the memories. After Chris moved out from Evelyn and Jake, he went to the lounge nearly every night.

He sat with his old buddies, the other regulars, and talked remember-when, shoulda-coulda, and if-only all night long. It was easier to talk here when there was nothing in particular to discuss. Chris would have his typical soda water and his friends would have their drink of choice: some would drink pop, others beer, and a few others hard liquors. Every night was the same, even down to the place's owner, Praeda. The tall Italian with jet-black hair and the shoulders of a former bodybuilder. He gave the same old sarcastic greeting, ribbing them about nursing drinks and never ordering enough food for a real bill.

One night, as Chris finished his walk by approaching the lounge, a particular memory of Evelyn came to mind. It was one of the simplest memories of her that stuck with him and he relived it as he approached the bar. The brief memory, where Evelyn touched his cheek then gave him a soft kiss before resting her head on his shoulder, came into his mind, and he embraced it willingly as he walked. It stayed with his thoughts as he flashed back, not realizing that he didn't turn left to enter the lounge. Instead, he walked straight ahead and eventually landed in the group meeting in the high school gym.

Chris hated the first meeting. His sponsor, Clara, was nice enough, but one of those perfect ladies who was so happy, it made you sick. Clara ran the group meetings and would immediately pull Chris into the group discussion portion. He forced himself to show up at least once a month. Evelyn would appreciate that he was trying. Clara urged him to show up more often, to be more engaged in the community to see the benefits. But in Chris's point-of-view, showing up twice a week to hear how others talk about their feelings, the impact their conditions had on their family, and their renewal to embrace their situation as a gift? Ugh. Chris tried not to be heartless but rolled his eyes in the dragged-out sessions every time someone made a quote-unquote *reborn breakthrough*, as Clara put it.

It shocked Chris to think it had been five years since his first visit; others had come and gone. They moved some that seemed to enjoy the sessions into other groups, and Chris lost track of them. Yet others who fidgeted and fussed the whole time gradually dropped out or moved into one-on-one sessions. Chris saw many of the dropouts at the lounge; they'd come and go, some angry and some sad with whatever troubles their conditions were causing, but all coming in to kill their time.

"So," Michael said as Chris sat in the surprisingly comfortable orange plastic chair, "What's on your mind?"

"Ummm," Chris stalled. He realized he was now one of those *types* moved from the group sessions into one-on-one coaching. He loved the idea of not having to listen to everyone else, but now he couldn't avoid the conversation. He couldn't hide his apathetic responses.

Michael waited patiently for Chris's answer as he smiled, not a huge grin but a welcoming soft smile that showed calmness and caring. The expression invited Chris into the conversation as the two locked eyes.

"Not to be rude," Chris broke eye contact, "but honestly, I wasn't thinking of anything."

"Yeah?" Michael questioned as his head dipped and he looked over his glasses at Chris.

"Yeah," Chris quickly responded.

Michael nodded in acceptance, comfortable in what Chris viewed as a terribly awkward silence.

Chris didn't admit it, but his actual thoughts were on how big Michael was. Praeda, who claimed to have won multiple European Strongman competitions in his younger days, was the most muscular person Chris knew. Michael did not have the obvious muscle definition of Praeda, but was at least 6'6" and solid as a rock, or maybe more like a small mountain. The glasses and button-up shirt took away from Michael's dominating physique, which rested under neatly trimmed salt and pepper hair and two-day stubble.

Finally, Chris broke the silence with his curiosity. "Why did I get moved from the group? How does that work?"

Michael's warm smile grew as he eyed Chris before responding, "To help those along who don't seem to respond to the group sessions."

"So you think I need help?" Chris asked.

"Everyone needs help, Mr. Flagler." Michael gave an inaudible laugh. "However, our organization's choice is to work here with limited resources. The group sessions work for many, but certainly not all, so here we are."

"Yes, here we are," Chris trailed off as his eyes wandered around the room. He saw the old gym bleachers, pushed up against the walls. The halls leading to locker rooms and restrooms were dark. Only the emergency lights, which always remained on in certain parts of the gymnasium, shined bright over Michael and Chris.

Michael looked Chris over, studying him as Chris continued to avoid eye contact. Then Michael broke the silence with a firm voice. "Why did you show up?"

"What?" Chris questioned, taken aback by the direct question. Clara was never so direct in the group sessions. "What do you mean, why did I show up? I want help with my condition. That's what you do, so I'm here."

Michael nodded with his gentle smile. "No, you don't."

Chris was confused. "What?"

"No, you don't want help," Michael clarified.

"I'm here, aren't I?" Chris stated in a defensive tone.

"I do appreciate that. In the end, simply showing up is a major part of victory. But there is more, and you are hiding," Michael said without changing the tone in his voice.

"Look, I'm here. What are we going to cover today? Can we talk about my memories and how to live with them?"

"We won't be talking about living with them," Michael replied matter-of-factly.

Chris was getting upset at how plainly Michael spoke. "And this is what we're covering; I want you to tell me why you came here today."

"I came because..." Chris's frustration mounted. "I want help with my condition, I'm sick and tired of not being able to..." Chris spoke bolder, losing his passiveness. "To talk to my son; to be with my wife. I...I...I WANT TO LIVE AGAIN!"

Michael's light smile turned into more of a grin, and it only ignited Chris further.

Chris stood up. "WHAT'S SO FUNNY?"

"Oh, not funny. I'm happy."

"You're happy that my life is in shambles and I get NO resolution by coming here. Good. Glad you are happy." Chris sat back down, feeling bad for snapping at his new sponsor at their first meeting. *Great way to start off,* he thought to himself.

Michael remained silent.

"Look, I'm sorry," Chris relented. "I haven't burst out like that before. I just don't know how to live with this anymore."

Michael's smile never waned during Chris's outburst. However, it seemed to fuel it.

"I think that is enough for today. Thank you for coming in."

Chris spun his head, making eye contact again. "WHAT? We just started!"

"It's not about the time, Christian. It's about the impact."

"Call me Chris," Chris responded, putting his hand up in a stopping motion. "No one calls me that anymore. And how am I supposed to live with this if we only talk for a minute?"

Michael politely stood up as Chris finished speaking. "I suggest you enjoy it while you can. And we won't be talking about living with your condition. We're going to talk about moving on despite it."

Michael bowed his head as his tall frame towered over Chris. "Until next time, Mr. Flagler." Then he strolled out of the dimly lit gym.

Thank You!

I hope you enjoyed the preview.

- Find it at https://store.jamesbonk.com/and enjoy a 15% discount with the code BESTSELLER when you buy directly from the author.

- You can stay in touch by signing up for my newsletter and getting special offers: https://hello.jamesbonk.com/signup/

Books By James Bonk

Light of the Ark Series

1. Light of the Ark

2. Shadows of the Ark

3. Light of the World

- Isaiah and the Sea of Darkness (standalone prequel)

More Fiction

- Christian's Look Back at Life

Stay up to date on new releases and email exclusive content: https://hello.jamesbonk.com/signup/

Acknowledgements

Thank you, Lord. None of this is possible without you.

My wife and daughters, for dealing with the extra time my mind spent in this world.

Leonard Petracci, for coaching me along this journey (*and for anyone who likes the Young Adult Sci-Fi / Urban Fantasy Genre, check out his work, especially the Star Child series*).

To Pastor Russ and my Life Group brothers at Southpoint Community Church, for helping me think through these topics via sermons and weekly discussions.

Photographer, Author Picture and Cover Model: Alicia Bonk (https://aliciabonk.com/)

Cover Art Designer: Jelena Gajic (zelengajic@gmail.com)

Editing (Proofing): Beth Lynne (https://www.bzhercules.com/index.html)

The Author

James Bonk writes Christian Fiction to develop his own faith and as a ministry. He lives in the North Atlanta area with his wife, two daughters, and fluffy Chartreux cat, Porkchop. When he's not writing, he's usually swimming or building forts with his girls!

His Light of the Ark book was the #1 New Release in its category upon release, with multiple five star reviews from adults and young adults alike.

Besides writing, parenting, and being a husband, James Bonk is a supply chain leader and business intelligence professional. He has a BS in Mechanical Engineering, MS in Industrial Engineering, and an MBA. He previously held his Professional Engineering license in Industrial Engineering.

Find out more at and get access to all his books at: https://store.jamesbonk.com/

You can also find James by searching James Bonk Author on your favorite platform or following the below links:

- Goodreads (https://www.goodreads.com/author/list/21997660.James_Bonk)

- Facebook (search '*James Bonk Author*' or go here: https://www.facebook.com/people/James-Bonk-Author/100092204034685/)

- BookBub (https://www.bookbub.com/profile/james-bonk)

The Author - James Bonk

Made in the USA
Monee, IL
14 January 2025

76898409R00125